Goose River Anthology, 2012

Edited by

Deborah J. Benner

Goose River Press
Waldoboro, Maine

Published by
Goose River Press
3400 Friendship Road
Waldoboro ME 04572
gooseriverpress@roadrunner.com
www.gooseriverpress.com

Table of Contents

Table of Contents

Table of Contents

Table of Contents

Table of Contents

In Memory of...

Scott J. Brooks

Philip Pendleton

Herb Coursen

Norma J. Crosier

Bentley Davis Seifer

Michael Rousseau

Palmer R. Cook
Cincinnati, OH

Mr. Willy Talks About Tonsils

Dad had an auto-repair-gas station-tires-and-batteries place that he ran himself. The front room was full of new tires, fan belts, and inner tubes. It always had the pungent aroma of new rubber. At the back of the building was a battery room that reeked of acid and ozone. A low, menacing buzz surrounded the batteries that squatted, black, wet, and corroded, on the charging bench. A workshop was sandwiched between the front room and the battery room and that was a truly a magic place for a six-year-old to listen and learn.

The workshop room was where tires were prepared for the retreading mold. Inner tubes for cars, boots for kids and waders for fishermen were all vulcanized on the same squeaky old, hot-press against its rear wall. Wheel rims were clamped on a tire-changing rack waiting for tires to be mounted on them with the help of hammers and pry bars and the like. A big coal furnace loomed in one corner of this magic place. In the winter, reeking of ashes and hot iron, it radiated waves of heat tempered with an occasional puff of coal smoke when the wind blew hard down the chimney, and the firebox door had round holes that glowed red like goblins' eyes when the damper plate was slid open. In the summer it sulked; its silent bulk threatening with its iron-rimmed eyes dark, swallowing any light that came near. Beside the furnace was an old car seat on a wooden box, a nail keg, and a folding chair, all meant to accommodate customers waiting for their tires to be fixed or for their cars to be repaired.

My dad was an affable teller of stories and discusser of local events. He talked as he worked, sometimes punctuating his comments by slinging a tool onto the hammers and pry bars that lay on a flat, wooden platform under the tire-changing rack in the center of the room. Quite a few of the visitors to that workshop room were there only to pass a lit-

Palmer R. Cook
Cincinnati, OH

tle time and tell, or hear, a story or two. I knew I could drift into this room and perch on the car seat, or chair, or nail keg, settle down with one of the tire trade journals or old *Time* magazines that were always about, and simply fade from everyone's attention. That was magic for me, and it was also a big part of my early, practical education.

After I got my nose into the pages of a tire trade journal or magazine the conversation, which waned when I showed up, would pick up again to its own natural rhythm. It was the house that burned the night before, or what the weather was doing to the crops, or who was caught again on drunk 'n disorderly. The story I remember best was told directly to me by Mr. Willy, one of Dad's regulars. I'm pretty sure he didn't own an automobile; he just often walked by and stopped to talk, which was okay, car or no car.

Mr. Willy was in his mid-sixties. He had a red, Irish nose and curly, pewter hair that curled all over his head, and he always wore mattress-ticking overalls with a plaid shirt. He was pleasant in a jolly sort of way, and he had bright blue eyes that sort of popped out, with one or the other of them looking at you while its companion drifted to the side in a most disconcerting manner. Unlike some visitors to my dad's workshop, he always said hello when I showed up and he always talked with me a little like I was a grown-up person even though I was only six. This particular day I told him about my tonsils being gone. The year was 1946.

"The doctor put a thing like a strainer over my face and it smelled funny and I got dizzy," I said. "Dad took me home, and it was too hot in the car, and my throat hurt. It hurt a lot and it was really sore for days."

He cleared his throat and fixed me with his monocular gaze. "Now you know," he said, "they aren't every going to grow back, which is, of course, a good thing. And since you've had done with them and won't ever have to have them out again, I'm going to tell you a story that happened at a house just over the railroad tracks and down the street.

Palmer R. Cook
Cincinnati, OH

"You know which house I mean," he said. It's just across from the one where I live only a little further along on this side of the street. It has a long, low front porch one step up from the sidewalk. You do know it now don't you, the one I'm speaking of?" He sat comfortably on the edge of the car seat, his hands on his knees with his fingers spread.

I settled on the nail keg, my least favorite seat because it had a sharp edge all around that cut into the back of your legs no matter how you sat on it. It had a tendency to tip the unwary especially if their feet didn't reach the floor. Looking up at Mr. Willy as I got my balance, I nodded.

"It's the one with an open lot beside it," he said, cocking his head at me and switching eyes to drive home his point. "It has an open lot beside it today, and it had an open lot beside it way back when this happened which was when I was just a boy not that much older than you are now. And that would be?" he said, just wanting to be sure I was focused on what he was saying.

"Six," I said.

"Yes, just so," he continued. "I was only a year or two or three ahead of that when this happened. At that time the house was owned by a man and his wife, and they had a little boy who was just about the same age as I was. And he wasn't a poor man. Everybody in town said he had money and he gave that little boy about everything he wanted.

"That man kept the grass mowed on that empty lot so's us boys, me and his son and some other boys of the same age here in town, could play football on it. And he used to go to the store and buy hard candy sticks that had different color stripes running up and around them like a barber pole. You know the kind I mean?"

I was ready for his question for I was onto his style of storytelling, so I nodded even though he seemed to be looking out the door toward the shadows the gas pumps cast on the hot driveway. I knew that he might be looking any which way, or maybe even in two ways at once with those bulgy,

Palmer R. Cook
Cincinnati, OH

drifting eyes, so I always judged his attention was in the direction his nose was pointing, even though I hadn't much certainty in the idea.

"Those candy sticks," he continued without acknowledging my nod, "had a little hole that ran right through the length of them, and his daddy would bring a bag of those candy sticks and a bag of lemons for us boys when we played football. When we got hot and tired and had to take a rest he would cut those lemons in half and give each of us one with a candy stick to suck the lemon juice through. 'Good for the throat,' he always told us, 'when you're hot from chasing a football.'

"Now there had been a big argument between him and his little boy," he said with just the slightest frown. "His daddy said he should have his tonsils out, and the boy was against it. And his mother, a little bit of a thing who always wore an apron and never said much, was quiet on the subject, although the boy told me she was on his side and was afraid to speak up.

"That day, which was hot and sunny, we was in the middle of our football game when the doctor, Doc Parsons it was, drove up in his one-horse, high wheeled rig."

The one-horse, high-wheeled rig caught my attention. In 1946 there was only one man in town, old Mike Briggs, who kept a horse, and he kept it to plow gardens in the spring and give carriage rides at fairs and such. And Mike only kept it to show off and make a little money and to keep his two boys busy carrying hay and shoveling out his garage where he kept the horse.

The mention of the doctor riding in a buggy made the time of Mr. Willy as a boy playing side-yard football recede far away from me like looking in the wrong end of a telescope. Mr. Willy must have known it too, for he looked at me and tapped me on the knee three times with his pointer finger.

"Listen up," he said. "Doc Parsons just swung out of that rig with his black bag and walked over and sat it on a table

Palmer R. Cook
Cincinnati, OH

right there on the porch near the front door. 'Which one?' he said. The boy's father said, 'He's the blue sweater with red stripes,' and he got up from where he was sitting on the end of the porch and strode right out amongst us boys, grabbing his son and lifting him up. The boy squirmed hard this way and that and kicked, but the only sound he made was a strained little groaning through his clenched lips that went umm-umm-umm. The rest of us boys just stood there rooted to the ground with our mouths agape, too scared to run.

'Put him over here, John,' the doctor said, motioning to the table on the porch. At the front door, silent behind the screen, was the dark shadow of the boy's mother, just a silhouette hidden by gloomy mesh. 'I'll hold him still if you'll just pour some chloroform on that cotton and hold it to his nose and mouth. It won't be a minute and he'll settle right down.'

"The doc was right," Mr. Willy continued, shaking his head. "That boy gave in, sighed and went right to sleep while the rest of the boys and I stood wide-eyed just at the edge of the porch. Then Doctor Parsons reached into his bag and started laying out, on a white towel, these silver tools like pliers and cutting things, and other items whose purposes we couldn't guess. That father sloshed more chloroform onto the cotton, keeping it wet and against the boy's nose and mouth while the doc sorted out his implements.

"Not one of us watching spoke or moved, especially not the silhouette hovering behind the screen door. The doc took off his coat and handed it to one of us boys to hold. Then he unbuttoned his cuffs and rolled up his shirt sleeves in a careful and deliberate way. Last, he reached into his black bag and took out a small pan and a white apron.

"Then, as he was putting that white apron on, the father looked up and said, 'Doc, his face is turned purple and now it's turning black. Is that the way it . . . .' "

"Oh, no man, the doctor said, and he slammed that bottle out of the father's hand and yanked the cotton off the

Palmer R. Cook
Cincinnati, OH

boy's face. 'You've killed him,' he shouted, and he grabbed the boy and shook that limp body like he could put life back in it."

Mr. Willy paused. "That chloroform bottle went spinning through the air, slinging the wet, stinking chemical all over us boys, and we ran off," he said. "After that there wasn't no more lemons, nor candy sticks, nor football, I never saw that boy's mother again, and I can't even so much as remember his name, neither first nor last." Mr Willy sighed heavily and shook his head. "You be glad boy, that your tonsils came out clean and slick as a whistle, cause things don't always work out thet-a-way." He heaved himself up off that old car-seat-on-a-box and headed toward the door. "No," he said without looking back at me sitting all stunned with the back of my legs hurting and the nail keg wobbling under me. "No, things don't always work out so good."

I watched Mr. Willy's broad back as he lumbered out the door and headed across the railroad tracks and down the street. Then I slipped off the nail keg and went outside. Dad had jacked a car up and was taking the lug nuts off one of the wheels. I listened to the screech of each nut as he loosened it, watched the whirling arms of his star wrench as he spun the nuts loose, and heard the klunk as he dropped each one from the wrench into the hubcap beside him.

"You're pretty quiet," he said over his shoulder as he gripped the tire, ready to pull it loose and drop it on the pavement. He paused and half-turned toward me. "I heard Mr. Willy start telling you about tonsils," he grinned. "He never gets tired of telling about when his tonsils were taken out. It happened at the house across from where he lives now. The funny part is that everything but the candy sticks and cut lemons changes every doggoned time he tells it." Dad pulled the tire off the car and rolled it across the sunlit drive toward the door where the tire-changing rack waited, and the sullen furnace sat watching in the cool darkness of the workshop.

Robert B. Moreland
Pleasant Prairie, WI

The Wall

In memory of Captain David Langston Coker, Jr.

The first time I saw the Wall,
it was in the chill of an early fall evening.
A sullen mist, a damp fog rolled in from Lincoln's feet.
The cold grey stone descended into the dark soil;
thousands of faces now chiseled names—forever young.

At the deepest point in the earth,
I found your name, tracing the letters with my finger
in vain hope of reaching out and embracing you.
To speak with you but a while, hear you laugh
and relive the memories, rich and vivid through the years.

I trace the letters of your name again,
think of when I last saw you at the height of summer.
And now in the cold darkness, you cannot see
me grieve for you and all the others as I remember
the lives not lived or children fathered, the sacrifices made.

The last time was in the late spring.
My son could not understand the names, the Wall.
So I told him of you, and when he asked why I was crying,
I traced again the letters of your name with my finger
and thought of you at the height of summer—forever young.

Moreland, R.B. and Miner, K.M. *Postcards from Baghdad:
Honoring America's Heroes.* Xlibris (Philadelphia, PA, 2008),
page 8.

Patricia Helmberger
Grand Rapids, MN

Touching Magic

Long ago when I was a child
And the world was magic,
I watched my mother make a patchwork quilt
And in the cold winter of a northern night,
It kept me warm.
In the darkness I would run my fingers over the patches
And know from which old shirt or dress each one was
        made.

The dusty rose velvet of my grandmother's skirt
And the checkered wool shirt my father bought
The day my brother came home from the war;
Mother's seersucker dress in aqua blue,
Her summer dress for church
Or walking to the lake in the afternoon.

The red and blue plaid of my twin sister's pleated skirts
Ordered from Sears in August for school in September,
And my own yellow cotton dress that I loved
And wore with white shoes and a little straw hat.

And when I touched them in the darkness,
I touched a magic world
With apple-scented grandmas,
Fathers with tears holding sailor sons,
Mothers with arms folding you against the world,
And sisters sharing secrets in the rain.

Mary Jo Balistreri
Waukesha, WI

Abby and the Light

She sits at the old cherry table,
socked feet curled around its center
pedestal just like her father did thirty
years ago. A bayberry candle flickers,
flames fantasies, fragments
that Abby scratches into form
on a yellow legal pad.
She sips hot chocolate, bites
down on a crunchy pretzel twist,
occasionally twines a strand of hair
around a finger, writing, always writing.

I sit with her reading *The Best
American Poetry, 2007,* but nothing stirs
me like this child. The slipping light
of late November illuminates
the small bent head, gathers itself around
her like a charm from the grief
she pours into a livable shape
for herself. It's Christmas and she wants
her brother back, will continue to write until
he comes alive on the page, until
the radiance she doesn't know she carries
enfolds them both.

Sally Belenardo
Branford, CT

Premonition

She liked the house for sale, but not the tree
across the street—an ancient maple
whose massive girth divided into limbs
twice the height of utility poles, its beauty
ruined by pruning to accommodate
power lines. It will fall in a hurricane,
she opined, obvious to anyone who doesn't
deny reality. Husband, not inclined to worry,

said the sturdy Cape was perfect for their needs—
which indeed it was, for ten years to the month,
before "Irene" crept up the coast.
The vast system, viewed from space
as a galaxy of cloud, aimed inevitably
their way. She eyed the tree...
its leaves shook in perpetual motion,
limbs slid back and forth against sky.

Onslaught of rain softened ground,
night fell. Weary from preparing,
husband slept in comfortable bed upstairs.
She hoped to survive in the cellar,
radio reporting likely tornadoes and storm's
progress. Next morning, wreckage strewn
around them, she was faced with the fact
the old tree and their house stood intact.

Nina M. Scott
Amherst, MA

Paying Forward

Aug. 26, 2009, was Jim's and my 48th wedding anniversary, and nowhere, in our opinion, was there a more perfect spot on the Maine coast to celebrate it than Harbor Island in Muscongus Bay. We can usually sail there in a bit over an hour, as our summer home and mooring are in Friendship.

While I packed a lunch (including biscuits for our sailing Lab, Kate) Jim readied our 28-foot Pearson Triton, *Caledonian,* and we got under way about 10 a.m. There was a bit more wind coming straight at us than we might have wished, so instead of tacking our guts out trying to get to Harbor Island, we opted for the "iron sail" and used the motor—not our preferred way of boating, but the point was to get there.

We did, and found the harbor almost completely deserted, which was unusual, as this is a popular destination for both local and visiting boaters. Dropping anchor, we first had lunch and then rowed ashore to give Kate her usual workout on the beach and some of the beautiful trails. This time she got so enthusiastic about exploring that she got separated from us. I stayed on the trail while Jim tracked her down, but the shrubs on the island were so dense that we could not reconvene until he had done some rock clambering and bushwhacking, resulting in a scraped ankle and scratched legs.

Kate's parents were not pleased with her. She, on the other hand, was delighted to see us. We called her an absolute ditz and headed for *Caledonian,* noting that while we were ashore about three other sailboats had moored in the sheltered waters of the harbor. We motored slowly out, exchanging waves with the other boaters, who also seemed to be on their lunch breaks, then hoisted sail, anticipating a number of exhilarating broad reaches on the way home.

In the middle of the narrow Black Island passage, we

Nina M. Scott
Amherst, MA

stopped dead in the water, having obviously snagged a lobster pot. This was the third time this had happened to us that season, and we were mystified why this was so, as *Caledonian* has a full keel and Jim had had a metal skeg attached to it to block the one vulnerable slot between keel and rudder. We are careful about lobster pots, but even if we sail over one, the line generally pops out from under our keel with no harm done. That said, there we were, broadside to the wind, and stuck, with an incoming tide and a building sea.

First things first: Drop the sails. Jim tried to motor in reverse to dislodge the line, but no go. We were also worried lest the pot warp get tangled in the prop blades. Jim got into our dinghy with the boathook to try to dislodge the line, but with the tide coming in there was too much tension for him to get the necessary slack to free us. Two lobsterboats were working near us, but too far away to hail.

After about 15 minutes of trying to free *Caledonian,* I noticed that two of the boats we had greeted were also leaving Harbor Island, and, seeing us immobile with sails in a heap on the deck, would surely come to our aid. We shouted and waved to them—and they passed us by. I was partly flabbergasted and partly outraged, as our experience has been that people on the sea come to the aid of others in trouble. We certainly always had, and had also received help from others. Not this time. A third sailboat went through the passage with the same result.

Jim changed into his bathing suit and got out goggles and knife, preparing to dive and cut the line. We live in a lobstering port, have fishermen friends, and know what their gear costs, so this is the last resort, but with no help in sight, it seemed the only thing to do. My skipper is now 72, though, and I was getting worried about his making like Jacques Cousteau.

At that point another lobsterboat appeared, and this one, to our great relief, headed determinedly for us. Her white bow

Nina M. Scott
Amherst, MA

bore the name *Debbie Jean,* and she was from Friendship. The skipper, who looked strong as a bear, had a blond young woman sterning. "Looks like you could use some help," the skipper said. We allowed as how we surely could.

"Hand me a bow line and let me spin you around," he suggested. With much churning water he did just that, but we were still stuck. I figured at that point that we had better get acquainted with our Good Samaritan, so we introduced ourselves to him.

"I'm Marty Benner, and this is my daughter Kasey," the skipper said. Kasey looked to be about 16 and obviously knew her way around a boat.

Marty took his gaff, hooked the offending line over his power winch, and turned it on. Not one but two nearby lobster buoys jiggled in the water.

"Looks like you got a two-fer," Marty observed. "That one over there belongs to my cousin. Well, we're going to have to cut the lines, but let's do it the right way." The winch whined as he pulled up the traps and put them on his deck. With a sharp knife he severed the tangled pot warp, and *Caledonian* immediately floated free. Gaffing the buoys, he put them on his deck as well.

"This way no one loses any gear," he smiled. I was still glad that it was Marty who had cut the lines and not we. After all, we're summer people and know the rules.

Jim and I were limp with relief and very grateful to the Benners. "What can we do for you, Marty, for helping us out?" I called to him.

"What you can do for me," he said, "is that the next time you see someone in trouble on the sea, you go and help them out." We promised to do so. *Debbie Jean* pulled away and we waved to Marty and Kasey as they got back to work.

"Wow," I said, equally in awe of his kindness and his seamanship.

We told the story of our rescue to a number of people, including our 93-year-old friend Marguerite Sylvester. She

Nina M. Scott
Amherst, MA

was originally "from away," too, but had lived in Friendship
for over seventy years and was a lobsterman's widow. She
knew Marty and said that he was a good man. "He was pay-
ing forward in what he asked of you," she observed, and
then, smiling, added, "you'll never forget this anniversary,
will you?" I owned that we would surely not.

***

I sent this story to *Points East* at the end of that summer,
and Nim Marsh said he would use it sometime in the future,
which happened to be August of 2011. He asked us to get
him a photo of the *Debbie Jean* with Marty and Kasey
aboard, which we were able to set up a few days ago. When
Marty expressed a wish to have the pictures, we used his wife
Debbie's e-mail address to send them over to him. It was
nice to renew contact with the Benners.

A few days later Jim and I got home about 7 PM, and I
happened to glance out of our front window, which overlooks
Friendship Harbor.

"What on earth is that green lobster boat doing out there
by the day beacon?" I said. "That's a terrible place to anchor
—it's right on top of some serious rocks. Thank God it's high
tide."

"I think it's dragging its mooring chain," Jim said, "and if
it keeps on going in this direction it might go on the rocks at
Ram Island. I'd better call the Harbormaster."

Fifteen minutes later a large Whaler churned out of the
harbor and up to the boat, somewhat ironically named
Almost There. Two men clambered aboard, hauled up the
parted chain, started the motor, and headed back down the
harbor. We were very relieved.

"How she ever threaded her way through the lobster fleet
without banging into someone is a miracle," Jim observed,
"especially with this wind honking out of the harbor."

Nina M. Scott
Amherst, MA

"I guess we did what Marty asked of us two years ago, didn't we?" I said.

"I was thinking the same thing," Jim replied.

But the story is not over yet.

The next morning we received an e-mail from Debbie Benner which really rocked us back on our heels:

"Thanks so much for the pictures but more importantly, thanks so much for spotting our son's boat drifting last night. Marty and Marcus wanted to call and thank you last night but we had a house full of people here for Kasey's graduation party...However, I'm sure you'll be hearing from them shortly. God works in mysterious ways—how appropriate that you be the ones to save us!"

As Marty observed later on the phone, "What goes around comes around."

The wise mother of a friend once put it like this: "Cast your bread upon the waters and hope it comes up sandwiches."

This time it surely did.

Nina Scott chairs the Amherst College Spanish Department. In the summers, she and Jim still sail *Caledonian,* their venerable Pearson Triton,in lobster-pot-filled Muscongus Bay.
First published in *Points East,* August, 2011.

*Editor's Note: I am the Debbie Benner mentioned and this is a true story!

Carol Leavitt Altieri
Madison, CT

My One-Room School

From scattered farms and villages, we
whisked to school in our yellow school bus,
clutching our black lunchboxes.

Ringing the bell, our teacher a juggler
balances five globes in the air: reading, writing,
multiplying, history and geography.

Pupils pledge allegiance with hands pressed
to hearts. Our teacher, a relic of sun and time
and roots of many backgrounds. Twenty-five

of us in eight grades learn in all-purpose
room protected from the autumn cold with a wood
fire in the stove kept burning by an older pupil.

A grandfather's clock ticktocks.

We all pitch in to help our school mates as clusters
of volunteers cycle one or two grades
at a time through lessons. *Why don't you go
to the blackboard to do your sums?*

A fifth grade boy pulls braids of a classmate.
A seventh grade has one boy going for his second time
        around.
Recess, mid morning, two grades let out early
as cows monitor the playground. We leap over the creek,
explore the pastures and woodland hills.
Pollen of goldenrod pervades the air.

Goose River Anthology, 2012//16

Carol Leavitt Altieri
Madison, CT

Thomas of the dunce cap catches a toad to scare the girls
as a snapping turtle seeks life in the swamp.
A black beauty horse is tethered outside waiting
to take our teacher home.
After school, we collect milkweed seedpods
for sailors' life preservers.
What if we all came back?
What would our voices say?

***

Sally Belenardo
Branford, CT

Apparition

On certain days
evenly spaced puffs of cloud
materialize
in a cloudless sky—
the exhalations of a leviathan
along the horizon
off Connecticut's coast—

and accumulate
in a linear formation, as air,
warmed more by a body of land
than the water around it,
rises and cools, condenses
into Long Island's
hovering ghost.

Goose River Anthology, 2012//17

Kay Prosser
Baraboo, WI

The Creek Society

I've never seen an otter
in Otter Creek
but golden marsh-marigolds
smother the banks
oozing blood roots
spill scarlet amidst green foliage
shy pink spring beauties peek—
watch out or you'll step on them—
purple and white violets
dark yellow trout lilies
common buttercups huddle against
hepaticas shining up from hairy stalks

cold, cold water bubbles
over slippery quartzite rocks
marking new channels
around winter blow downs
frail flowers clutch bank edges
clinging together against April wind
hugging each other along Otter Creek
sharing their haven in the woods

Sherry Ballou Hanson
Brunswick, ME

Outside Bar Harbor

Sun tracks on a silver sea
as great white clouds mass
above sloping ledges
taking what warmth they can
from this tentative September day.

Off shore the channel buoy
tolls a warning to lobstermen
hauling traps, a north wind has come

stirring the salt sea aroma
and essence of balsam fir,
catching waves and lifting white caps,
spreading arcs of foam
to mix with glitter on the water.

Time is fleeting.

***

Daniel Jamieson
Candler, NC

You, there...

You will never love!
    Love is an irrational impulse;
you're a solipsist, too cerebral
    to experience a natural instinct
—such as loving another person.

Goose River Anthology, 2012//19

Helene McGlauflin
Bath, ME

Mother's Day Without You

We have shared five hundred million moments
have missed millions of moments since,
will miss a billion moments more

Mysteries of my womb
remember me sometimes, won't you
when you see a newborn, find a lullaby hidden
in a sweet secret place I tucked in long ago,
when you sew a button on a shirt with ease
cook a meal, go to bed early, or feel yourself
planted firmly on earth, instinctively sensing only
hurricane force could knock you down, when
you give love, see love, find love, know love
then I will know our shared moments mattered

Think of me sometimes, won't you,
when you crave, pour, then savor a cup of tea
plant a marigold seed in a small cup, smile seeing
bluets shivering as breeze passes through grass in May
climb a mountain and during that final push to summit
feel the heart that once shared a cadence with mine
beating hard with the affirmation: alive, alive, alive
or look at stars, know them as yourself continually
shining for light years though surrounded by black space
then may there be millions less one I have missed

Helene McGlauflin
Bath, ME

Call me sometimes, won't you
when I can still offer something you need or you
want to share with the certainty that I will care
if ever you feel unloved, abandoned or afraid and seek
the comfort of an old sweater, a poached egg, an ocean
      breeze
when you have time for a meandering conversation that
      strolls
in a place so familiar it recurs in a dream, or on the day
you know a loneliness deep in your core creating an
inexplicable yearning that only a long known voice can
      soothe
then may there be billions less one we will share

***

Liz Moser
Baltimore, MD

On Learning of a Cancer Diagnosis

I am suddenly reduced to the sum of my parts,
no more adventuring, expansions into other ways and
      places.
I must consolidate, pick up my pieces, make order out of
scattered papers, empty files and outworn shoes and
      sweaters.
My calendar is full of dates and question marks I must
      erase, call off,
decide who needs to know I'm unavailable
      indefinitely.

Goose River Anthology, 2012//21

Bentley Davis Seifer
Burlington, VT

Dandelions

Burning yellow flowers
All across the endless field.
First you're beautiful,
And then, "poof"
you're gone.

***

Evening Star

You bring back sheep from their grazing place
You bring back cats from their morning walk
You bring back the dark.

***

Racoons

Scurrying, scurrying, scavenging
Scavenging, scavenging, scurrying
Looking about the dark night
A loaded trash can
Nobody around
Riiiiip! Glorious.
Away it goes carrying all it can
A true bandit with a mask.

Bentley Davis Seifer
1998-2011
RIP

Goose River Anthology, 2012//22

Janice Babcock
Wauwatosa, WI

Bye, Bye Boss!

My father and I headed off to the seed store just before Easter. I was so excited. Imagine, the owners were offering those cute chicks for free! This adventure was common for the area children in our small town. I begged to have my very own chicks, and Dad couldn't say no to his eight year old daughter. When I brought them into our house, I could see my mom was not thrilled. But when she saw my excitement, she reluctantly said yes.

Wow! The chicks could stay!

Mom explored what was available to house our new boarders. Mom and Dad quickly pooled their creativity to make a brooder for warming the six little chicks. Dad found a sturdy wood box in the basement. My mom rummaged through the Christmas supplies. She draped Christmas tree lights around the top of the box. *Voila!* The babies had a warm home in our kitchen. My responsibility for the new chicks included feeding and nurturing them.

I noted that one chick was in charge. While the others were bedded down for the night, the self-appointed Boss stood on one leg with the other comfortably tucked under his wing. He also mysteriously kept one eye open to protect the others from any intruder.

Later, my father made wood chips for a new enlarged cage he now put in the basement. I kept that pen clean. Over a short time, we introduced these city chicks to the world outside the basement. At first the young ones were frightened when they walked on the grass in our yard. I think it tickled their breasts. Everything was new to them, including the sunlight, blue sky and a slight breeze. The Boss haughtily pranced around their expanded afternoon domain.

While my chicks were maturing, Pooky, my classmate who lived two houses away was having some problems.

Janice Babcock
Wauwatosa, WI

Pooky's mom approached my mom regarding his chicks. She said that a few of his chicks had died. She begged us to take over the remaining ones. Our answer was yes. Now I had even more responsibility including, feeding more chicks and cleaning their smelly cage. However, I could meet the challenge!

One Sunday some Racine Dominican nuns, who were my school teachers, strolled past our house and saw my chicks outside. I was thrilled to show the little ones off. For me, it was like "show and tell." I explained how I was given the chicks. I felt like I was their mom because I could hold my yellow babies, feed and care for them. The nuns smiled with encouragement to me.

Eventually, Easter was well behind us and it was now time for my city roosters and laying hens to leave their home. They were getting too big to keep in our basement. I was sad to see them go. Dad, Mom and I drove them to New Fane, near Kewaskum, to Grandma and Grandpa's house. They had their own flock of chickens.

When my chickens were intermingled with my grandparent's flock, Grandma immediately picked out my Boss rooster by his dominant behavior. I was later told that he was very aggressive toward Grandma. She took him by the neck and twirled him around. Yipes! She did not kill him, but that showed who was in charge of her chicken coop!

When I visited some time later the flock was smaller. Some chickens were butchered when fully matured. I was never told when we had chicken dinner if it was one of my original chicks. However, regarding the notable rooster, I knew the inevitable would happen to him. "Bye, Bye Boss!"

Tyler B. Richards
Edgecomb, ME

A Hunter's Morning

Dawn is setting on the horizon,
Colors of yellow, orange and red touch the treetops.
Grey lifts from the ground,
Frost gives way to cool, crisp fall air.

The world is not yet alive,
The sky has yet to turn blue, clouds white.
Scenery is black and white,
Shadows are dark, deep, mysterious.

Birds begin to sing
Attempting to coax the green back into their homes.
In the distance a low hum
As a fisherman starts his boat on the river.

This is a hunter's morning.
When only those outside before daybreak
Can honestly say that they
Experienced a Maine morning.

A few hundred yards away
The field is touched with gold, revealing
A small herd of deer
Feeding on grasses, acorns and clover.

From his place on the foundation
The hunter watches them closely as the
World around him springs to life.
The fisherman opens the throttle.

Now late in the morning
The hunter is satisfied.
He has had his time with nature,
And that of him no one can deprive.

Russell Buker
Calais, ME

Bread

I miss
the tree that was at my
window
and the staring contests with
big red
the stock-still squirrel

Now
I am able to shake
hands
with the red rash of my
mornings
unable to feel the waving

winds
and rains nor place those
crusts
of expected amazement
felt
watching Red's bobbing

cheeks
and cold eyes on me
as if
I was more or less his
reluctant
savior, mostly less

now
that the tree has been
taken
down by wind and rain
and I
had to cut it up for removal

Goose River Anthology, 2012//26

Earl Weigelt
Winslow, ME

The Gritty Annoyances

So, riddle me this…

I think I get the Big Ones,
the loss and pain and grief.
It's the little things that strike me dumb,
that leave me asking "Why?"

It's the mechanical break;
the forgotten thing;
the nagging hip and throbbing back;
that nasty black ice patch;

The thigh-deep slush on Eagle Lake;
the white caps on Caucomgomoc;
The rod tip in the tailgate;
and the auger that won't start!

The license on the bedroom floor—
the Warden at my pickup door;
the hole in the net; my missing vest,
and my maps left in the drawer!

I wonder if it's conspiracy,
or if all the blame belongs to me.
But no matter what, I won't quit!
I must get outside…and I will!

And perhaps in His mercy
when the Almighty takes me,
He'll let me in on the joke.

Goose River Anthology, 2012//27

Diane Reitz
Winter Park, FL

The Brass Lantern

The brass lantern
so dimly lit,
barely seen
across the pond

The lantern is lit
each night in hope
of a returning soul

The lantern mails
its beam across
the pond—searching
for its lost heart

From a night
long ago when
there was no returning
from the sea

Wind gently swaying
the lantern and
the porch swing in
an afternoon lullaby

The sun bouncing
off the brass and
the glass—blinding
the sky

Diane Reitz
Winter Park, FL

Until the fog rolls in—
a ghost changing
shape—the lantern's
light reaching out

Working harder
on a stormy night
to comfort and become
a reacquainted friend

A stationary point
from which a message
is sent—of hope—as
is kept near the heart of

The brass lantern

***

Patricia Helmberger
Grand Rapids, MN

A Holy Place

"Turn the canoe around," I whispered,
"We are intruding."
We had frightened the frogs from their lily pads,
The turtles from their ancient logs,
And the red-winged blackbird from its reed.
We turned around, feeling ashamed
As one would feel
Having walked shouting into a church.

Goose River Anthology, 2012//29

Lou Roach
Poynette, WI

Sea Change

The smallest bits of living
shape so much of every day.
Unplanned hours allow freedom
to consider pursuits to enhance
these retrospective years, not just
fill them with doing "make work."

Ideas once forgotten nudge us
to look beyond ourselves—
to reach to those we hurried past
when ambition, accomplishment
and raucous rides to a career
left us alone traveling the fast track.

We still have time to do things left undone—
to speak those words just begging to be said,
to listen closely when others ask,
to be more patient, show compassion—
simple acts, remembered soon enough,
we hope, to deserve this gift of time.

Juliana L'Heureux
Topsham, ME

Racing Over Adversity: Meeting Ron Turcotte

I'm not an autograph collector, but the signature I own from Ron Turcotte is a particular treasure. Turcotte is a horse racing Triple Crown hero who exceeded my expectations after we met, because he exposed a life beyond the dream of winning equestrian victories.

Turcotte is rare among an elite group of racing champions. He won back to back races at the Kentucky Derby in 1972 and 1973. Then, in 1973, riding Secretariat, he made horse racing history by winning the Triple Crown.

Turcotte and Secretariat were an impressive racing duo. Together, they won the Kentucky Derby at Churchill Downs, the Preakness at Pimlico, in Baltimore Maryland and the Belmont Stakes in New York during the same year. It's an extraordinarily difficult feat for one horse and jockey to win all three races. In fact, some sports writers called Secretariat "the super horse of the 19th century," because of his ability to sustain his strength through the end of his winning races.

Being a world famous jockey is heroic enough, but Turcotte became a champion after acquiring a disability in 1978, the result of an accident at the Belmont. Since then, he's been a paraplegic, meaning the injury caused him to lose mobility in his legs. His heroism shines in the quietly professional way he expresses a profound appreciation for his life *after* acquiring a disability. Moreover, he's become a motivational speaker for disabled jockeys and a role model for all who overcome physical challenges.

My meeting with Turcotte followed more than a decade writing about him as a news reporter for Maine's French-Canadian and Franco-American cultures (33 percent of the state's population shares these ancestries). He was born on July 21, 1941, one of eleven siblings. He grew up in a close knit French speaking family, in Drummond, New Brunswick, Canada. His father worked in the Northern woods as a log-

Juliana L'Heureux
Topsham, ME

ger. Turcotte left school after finishing the 8th grade to work with his father in logging, but his small size kept him out of the rugged side of the job. Instead, his job as a teenager was caring for the logging camp's horses. Although he was too small for forestry work, his physical attributes made him a perfect fit for horse racing.

Eventually, Turcotte learned to work with race horses, which clearly led him to become a jockey. In one interview I had with him, he acknowledged his "horse whisperer" talent for treating horses with gentle tactics and speech.

Computer search engines typically find my name when people start looking for the Triple Crown winners of horse racing. My byline pops up around the first Tuesday in May, when Kentucky Derby followers look for past winners. Turcotte is one of eleven jockeys since 1919, to win the Triple Crown.

Turcotte rode in 20,281 races in his career, beginning in 1961. By the premature end of his career in 1978, he won first place in 3,021 races (including riding Riva Ridge in the 1972 Kentucky Derby and Belmont Stakes). He placed 2nd in 2,897 and showed 3rd in 2,559 races, with a total recorded $29,606,205 winnings in his career.

Numerous accolades and honors are included in his resume. He is an esteemed member of several Halls of Fame, including The Canadian All Sports Hall of Fame. Sculptor Edwin Bogucki created a statue at Churchill Downs featuring Turcotte, riding Secretariat immediately after the Kentucky Derby on May 5, 1973, as he danced into the winner's circle, led by his groom Eddie Sweat.

Every May, Turcotte is a guest of the Kentucky Derby.

Queries about how to find Turcotte come from sports magazines, television anchors, curious readers and children. An 11 year old 6th grader from Upstate New York asked her grandmother to call me about how she might contact Ron Turcotte? In her case, she wanted to ask Turcotte how to find the jockey clothing like he wore in 1973, when he rode

Juliana L'Heureux
Topsham, ME

Secretariat to the Triple Crown victory. She wanted to role play his winning story to her school class.

Responding to her request, Turcotte went beyond speaking with this young fan on the phone. He even took time to write a short autobiography called "My Personal Story," so she could read it during show and tell, while wearing the racing attire.

He wrote to her about his faith in God and the "ups and downs" of his racing career. "I had some great wins and some disappointments, but through it all, I have always tried to give it my best," he writes.

Furthermore, he writes, "I had a chance to ride some top horses and win some major stakes, but 1972 and 1973 were, of course, the highlights. Riding Riva Ridge and Secretariat gave me the biggest thrills, winning two consecutive Derbies, which had not been done in 71 years. Then, of course, the honor of winning the Triple Crown."

"Although I had a racing spill in 1978 that put an end to that part of my life, I am now a paraplegic, confined to a wheel chair. But, I don't consider my life to be over by any means. I was lucky to have the full support of my family and was able to come back to Canada and lead a rich, fulfilling life with my wife and four daughters. My wife, who comes from Drummond, New Brunswick, where I grew up, shares the same principles we instilled in our children and that our parents taught to us. We believe life is not always easy, but it is what you make of it. (Moreover)...my injury gave me the chance to really enjoy more time with my family and to spend precious time with my parents," he writes.

My personal meeting with Turcotte was finally realized when he happened to be speaking in Waterville, Maine, at a venue called The Muskie Center. A group of Senior Spectrum community members asked if he would speak at a fund raising event. At the time, his cousin was driving him north to his home in New Brunswick, so he agreed to stop overnight, for the opportunity to speak.

Juliana L'Heureux
Topsham, ME

Many of the adults brought their grandchildren to hear Turcotte speak. These children seated themselves cross legged on the floor, forming an arc around the base of his wheel chair. A standing room only crowd filled the room and lined up along the walls.

Initially, I thought meeting Turcotte would allow me to hear some interesting horse racing stories. Maybe I'd even get an autograph. After more than a decade of periodically speaking with him on the phone while covering his biography as a French-Canadian son of a lumber jack who became an icon of the French-Canadian sports culture, I assumed there was little else to learn about his many accomplishments.

But, I was wrong.

On first impression, he appears shy, but his capacity to charm quickly infected the room. His smile beamed through a calm demeanor. You get the sense of how he must have had a calming effect on high strung racing horses.

Wearing a casual executive suit, he looked completely different than the real life jockey actor Otto Thorwarth, who played Turcotte in the popular Disney released movie *Secretariat.*

Turcotte showed videos of his horse racing victories. Having him personally explain the details of each individual Triple Crown win, while showing videos riding Secretariat was nearly as exciting as being at the track. He explained what was going on with detailed descriptions of the race, like the events happened yesterday. He's justifiably pleased to show the video of Secretariat's Belmont win, the third leg of the Triple Crown. That's the arduous race where he won, with Secretariat, by 45 lengths, a record that's yet to be broken.

Spontaneous applause followed each video, especially when the audience saw Turcotte edging out other horses while appearing to fly toward the finish lines.

As the audience cheered each race, a jovial Turcotte seemed to take on the energy of where he was in the videos.

Juliana L'Heureux
Topsham, ME

He looked like he could let go of his wheel chair in a second, if someone just put him in the saddle of another race horse.

My brief meeting with Turcotte returned more than stories or a souvenir autograph. I gained an understanding about what makes Turcotte a hero. It's a character trait he projects when speaking about the totality of his life, particularly his response to the adversity he experienced during his physical and career changing challenges.

An audience member in Waterville asked Turcotte how he felt about his life changing disabling injury. Turcotte gave a typically optimistic response: "I don't think of myself as being disabled," he said. "I believe God has granted me the ability to live a wonderful life."

Turcotte and his wife Gae live in Grand Falls, New Brunswick, Canada. It's a long way from almost anyplace you can name, but only a phone call away from his many fans. In fact, it's been my experience that he and Gae answer all phone calls and email.

Secretariat and Turcotte visited several times after both their racing careers ended. "He came up to me when I whistled," he told the Waterville audience. Secretariat died at Claiborne Farms, in Paris, Kentucky, on October 4, 1989, after suffering from a treatable but incurable laminitis, an inflammation of the hoof.

Finishing his education was another milestone Turcotte accomplished in May, 1990, when he earned a high school diploma from Caribou High School, in Maine.

An authorized biography, currently out of print, about Turcotte's life, with stories from his childhood in the logging camp and his career, was told to sports writer Bill Heller (with Ron Turcotte). *The Will to Win: Ron Turcotte's Ride to Glory,* was published in 1992, by Fifth House Publishers, in Saskatchewan Canada. I've encourage a reprint of this inspiring memoir, especially since the movie *Secretariat* was so popular.

Turcotte's faith in God inspired him to persevere through

Juliana L'Heureux
Topsham, ME

his "ups and downs." Yet, beyond his personal story, he inspired those who met him in Waterville, Maine to think optimistically about how people living with disabilities are able to be role models for all of us.

Turcotte's victorious stories lifted the mood of his audience while he practically hypnotized the children with the personal accounts of his winning races.

Everyone there saw and heard a real hero.

Obviously, my Ron Turcotte autograph is now more than a souvenir.

It's symbolic of how a determined human spirit can race over adversity.

***

Marilyn Zelke-Windau
Sheboygan Falls, WI

Hibernation

If bears are hibernating, don't go in the cave.
Don't awaken a sleeping ursine who's supine.
They like to clawhog the bedcover,
winter side up.
They drooldrip off swollen purple tongues.
Their crack-lidded eyes reveal no revels,
only bloodshot basins and brown.
Their mat their matted fur,
lump spot, mud crusted.
They roll toward spring
without benefit of Serta,
certain in honey dreams of
blackberry stains.

sarah p. roy
Oakland, ME

Remember

From the small white dilapidated
building she runs,
torn and bruised—
her outside shell intact.

On this cool night of no wind,
she walks fast without wings.
Rain's rhythm becomes
her fragile heartbeat.

In early morning's shadow
of gold and red dripping leaves,
she hears a
mighty engine's call . . .

With the sun's coming after rain,
in glorious colors of autumn,
she remembers this one truth—

trains run on time.

Katrina Ireland
Brewer, ME

Blood Lines

Blood is thicker than water. That adage may be true,
But it takes more to hold a family together, for blood, it
      isn't glue.
Please heed my words. Open your eyes to see.
In order to keep the roots alive within the family tree,

Just as a sapling, to become a strong and sturdy oak,
It requires watering and nurturing, not merely feeble hope.
Blood is thicker than water, but let your ears hear the
      truth.
It takes more to keep a family together, for blood, it isn't
      glue.

Biology gives us characteristics as in the color of our hair
      and eyes,
The shape of our noses, our structure, and our size.
Blood carries nutrients to the body, but in order for us to
      become whole,
We also need nourishment to feed the light which dwells
      within our soul.

We are all from a larger family since the beginning of
      mankind,
Connected through biology and grafted in our Father's vine.
Our blood lines are important. That, I agree is true.
But, the love of God's spirit, my friends, is the binding glue.

Diane H. Schetky
Topsham, ME

Golfing in Pangnirtung

Pangnirtung is the arts capital of Baffin Island in the territory of Nunavut. The village is situated on a fjord at the lower tip of the island between Cumberland Sound and Davis Strait. If one travels further east, the next point of land would be Greenland. It is not exactly a destination point for your average traveler. Disembarking from our vessel, a Russian icebreaker, our party dispersed to explore Pangnirtung on foot. We toured the print-making center and admired beautiful works of Inuit art. We conversed, ate with the local people and joined them in a game of cricket. Along the sidelines, I noted several youths swinging golf clubs but no golf balls.

As I climbed the bluff to admire the view of the fjord and snow capped mountains, I came across yet another young boy carrying a golf club. I struck up a conversation with him and he told me that his name was Scott. I replied that I had a son named Scott. I asked about the golf clubs. He said there were many on the island, left behind by a tourist. He lamented the fact that they had golf clubs but no longer had any golf balls. He noted the one store in the village did not stock golf balls. He then offered to show me the town golf course. We climbed a bit higher to a plateau where he proudly pointed out a large piece of canvas tacked down on four corners with a tin can sunk in the middle. In as much as grass does not grow here, I admired their ingenuity. I immediately surmised why there were no longer any golf balls. The temptation to whack a ball into the fjord must be irresistible. As I looked out into the fjord, I saw yet another unexpected sight, someone water skiing in a red wetsuit in these arctic waters. Pangnirtung was full of surprises.

I told my new friend, Scott, that I would send him some golf balls when I got home. He beamed. On my way home, I was stalled at Newark Airport for eight hours due to weather. I had plenty of time to search for golf balls and found

Diane H. Schetky
Topsham, ME

some with bright yellow New York City taxi and police logos on them. I bought a set, hoping they would be visible on snowy Baffin Island, and sent them off to Scott.

A few months later, I received a thank you note from Scott's mother. She apologized for not having him write but explained that Scott was a bit slow and that she and her husband were in the process of adopting him. He'd come from another community where he had been abused and had been having difficulty adjusting to his new life in Pangnirtung. She explained that Scott was not his given name but his nickname, which was easier to pronounce than his Inuit name. Ever since he received the golf balls, all the children in the village now wanted to play with him. His new mother rejoiced everyday upon seeing him come home with wet and muddy shoes from having been out playing with new friends. She thanked me for my kindness and added a PS saying she was the village social worker.

I expect the New York City golf balls have now joined all the others at the bottom of the fjord. They have served their purpose. A golf ball can have a big ripple effect.

***

Steve Troyanovich
Florence, NJ

still the leaves fall...and dream

your lips became my blanket
your body covered my dreams...
beyond all the shadowed landscapes
i have glimpsed
the cosmic autumn
of your being

Gerry Rita Di Gesu
West Chatham, MA

Hibiscus

Will Kevin succeed in his new job? Will Chris finally get the financing for the business? Will Nancy get the job she applied for today? Thoughts of my children whirl around in my head as I sit down for a cup of tea at the kitchen table. Adult children who can take care of themselves. But when you love, how do you stop worrying about them, stop waiting for them to be "settled?"

As I sit at the table, my eyes wander toward the large hibiscus plant on the floor next to me. Gazing at the glory of the scarlet flower which opened this morning and thinking about its brief life cycle, I remember again God's perfect order in nature, proof of His design in our lives—a reminder life happens in His time, not mine.

The hibiscus bud forms slowly, swelling to become a pink embryo which is born one glorious morning in shades of crimson and yellow. It lives a full life in this one day, dancing in the sunlight and bringing joy. I nod and smile each time I gently touch it, acknowledging the peace with which it fills me. Then it rests overnight, still in full bloom.

The following morning, imperceptibly, one at a time, the five petals start slowly to turn back inward toward their core. It is this gradual folding inward of each petal that again reminds me to try to see and accept life on a daily basis without worrying about the future. I'm aware as I pass the plant through the course of the day that not all petals close at the same pace, as the stages of different lives are not measured evenly. We come into the world full of life and promise. The years progress and we become all we can be by filling our days yet always reaching toward the next. Then, aging slowly, we turn inward as gently as the petal turns inward to rest.

Another night passes and in the morning the bud has slipped off its stem and rests on the floor. I pick it up and notice how tightly the petals have closed around each other, their job finished. Gently I set it in the yard under oak leaves so it may return to the earth.

Genie Dailey
Jefferson, ME

Bold Coast Day

Not quite daylight . . .
I wake to the rumble of lobster boats
        rising and falling on morning swells.
With eyes still closed, it becomes a game
            to single out differing engine sounds . . .
How many fishermen working the waves today?

Gradual brightening . . .
I become aware of other morning noises,
            a quiet symphony of earth and life around me:
The whistles and twitters of birds and squirrels;
The bong of a buoy, the cry of a gull;
            snickering branches with shuffling leaves
            and chuckling cobbles nearby on the beach.

Full sunshine now . . .
I'm out at the tideline watching the whitecaps
            curling and cresting, diving and dancing.
The pulse of the sea is the soul of the place;
I spend my day drifting, just looking and listening.

Deepening twilight . . .
The tangerine moon rises up from the sea
            and the startled stars retreat a little.
I kindle a campfire encircled with shore stones.
The rocks and the wood, the smooth and the rough,
            seem to reflect the moods of the ocean,
            the rhythms of life.

Wood and water;
            sky and stone, sun and moon, wind and fire;
            solitude
            and friends.

Lynne O'Leary Annis
Rockport, ME

A Librarian Notices You

I can see you mean it—
Your eyes look different.
Something beyond the surface,
I can feel it.

I want to take away your pain,
But there are parts of you I don't know.
I can't get in there,
I don't have the right to.

But I wish for you the happiness
That I would give you if I could—
Wrapped in a shiny package
Just for you.

Can I help you up?
Pretend I don't notice your sadness?
I am sending you a warm embrace
As you walk by me.

I said a little prayer
Underneath my breath
That you will be okay,
When you walked past.

You waited for a ride just outside the door,
I watched you get in the car.
But once you left, I was still stuck
Looking at your pain.

Jean Lawrence
Waldoboro, ME

On the Day You Left Us

On the early spring morn that you left us, birds' chirps of
      joy awoke me as dawn appeared.
Later, as I raked brittle leaves and dried weeds from the
      house gardens,
         spiked leaves and buds of daffodils came into view.
Waking from their long winter's sleep, crocus blossoms
      dotted the edge of the lawn
         cheering me in my uncovering tasks.
Debris fallen from trees during a recent windstorm was
      raked from the hill,
         and a cardinal sang nearby.
Breezes whispered softly through the old pasture pines,
      as I ambled about the yard
         observing buds on azaleas and rhododendrons.
I heard and saw Nature celebrating as I knelt in the warm
      garden soil to weed.
New life, abundant and free, was everywhere on the day
      you left us.
All creation rejoiced in your dawn victory over death!

Karen Lewis Foley
Topsham, ME

Tsunami

Coffee cup in sunlight
set upon tablet on table,
shifts shapes of white
ceramic shadows and light.

Steam curls off the dark lake.
Somewhere ocean water rocks,
hauled by continental quake,
travels days beyond the ache

of heaving rock and broken bone
above, while underwater
born, by earthforce honed,
the tsunami surges home.

By the window here, this
ceramic hemisphere in hand,
the oak leaves shine and toss
in lifting wind, the brass

grasshopper vane turns.
Half a world beyond the lake
the earth and sea subside, the dead yearn
for nothing, the stricken living mourn.

Mollie Schmidt
Rome, ME

Awake at Night

Awake at night
I listen to the loons,
their speech so rich and varied:
crooning, moaning, then
ridiculous arpeggios
of raucous squawks—

I would I could express
like them the intensity
of my relationships,
summing up past griefs,
present loves, the pain
of living over, under water;

beneath, I dream and float,
no touch save water,
soundless, striving to
name each growing
plant or child, a deep
regret for the singer I once could be.

Rosemarie Nervelle
Camden, ME

Magnolia Street

The Sheppard family was once one of the oldest and most financially stable families in Atlanta, Georgia. The Sheppard Plantation was probably the largest and most successful in the state. They were also a family of political importance. Senators and legislators gathered privately at the Sheppard home to discuss war strategies when they realized the war was going badly for the South. It was said that Robert E. Lee once spent a night at the Sheppard home on Magnolia Street just before the attack on Atlanta by General Sherman in 1864.

Rodney J. Sheppard, Sr., a proud, young cotton baron of considerable family wealth, survived the devastating destruction of the war. The plantation was spared; his town house and grounds in the city, however, sustained considerable damage when Sherman's fires reached that section of Atlanta. Sheppard, like so many other homeowners in the neighborhood, was financially able to rebuild after the war. The Sheppard property on Magnolia Street bloomed again in a neighborhood of stately old homes, manicured lawns, ancient magnolia trees and magnificent gardens; a show-place of gentility and excellent taste. Rodney raised a family of five boys, a proud progeny of Sheppard family males, all well-educated and successful.

Rodney J. Sheppard, Jr., the youngest of the third generation, was born in that brilliantly white, palatial home in 1923. He nostalgically remembered the "twenties," when he, just a small boy, watched from between the balustrades of the grand staircase as the dancers glided over the ballroom floor. The Sheppard family was the toast of the town, hosting formal parties, cotillions and political gatherings. The ladies danced the Charleston, the rage of the times, in glittering jeweled headbands and beaded dresses that swayed with the movement of their slender hips, their stockings rolled down

Rosemarie Nervelle
Camden, ME

just below the knee, showing the white flesh of their thighs. Oh, Magnolia Street glowed in its heyday! Rolls-Royces, Stutz Bearcats and Morgans lined the circular driveways where chauffeurs awaited their employers' departure from gentile garden parties and posh soirees which lasted far into the night. Those were the days! And Rodney, Jr. yearned for his youth when he was happier than any other time he could remember. The Great Depression of the 1930s brought an end to life as the Sheppards and their affluent neighbors had known it. Three brothers of the current Sheppard clan with young families were forced to move back to the homestead. Against Rodney's will, they divided the huge house into apartments to suit their needs and rode out the lean years. To Rodney, this was an insult to his aesthetic sensibilities. Prohibition provided Rodney's brothers the means to make big and fast money. One by one, they moved out and reestablished themselves in their own homes and businesses elsewhere in the city. He felt well rid and cared not that his brothers were involved in illicit business dealings.

Rodney Sheppard, Jr., the youngest of four brothers, was a slightly built, impeccably groomed bachelor in his early fifties who lived privately in his own quarters, angrily watching the neighborhood change over the years. He resented the 1970s with its rock 'n roll music, its crude television programming, and its youthful, scornful disregard for parental respect and guidance.

When his parents died, Rodney bought out his brothers' shares and decided to restore the house to its original splendor, hoping the neighborhood's older residents would follow suit, as they had when his great, grandfather rebuilt his house many years before. He had hoped that his actions would encourage his neighbors to feel confident that their real estate values would rebound.

It took a little more than two years and most of Rodney's inheritance to restore the family home. But, he was completely happy with the results. Tall white columns stood like

Rosemarie Nervelle
Camden, ME

sentinels on the grand veranda, the house's fenestrations, doors, and moldings were restored to their original grandeur. The grounds had been magnificently groomed with English ivy, boxwood, exotic trees, rose gardens and a lily pond. Although the inside renovations had been kept private, he threw a grand open-house party and invited everyone on Magnolia Street. He stood back and admired the fruits of his investment, and felt that he had honored his progeny as well as having displayed his own impeccable taste. Rodney's importance in the community took on a whole new meaning when the house was finished. His neighbors looked up to him and sought his financial advice when—and if—they decided to restore their own homes.

Rodney enjoyed several more satisfying years in his beautiful surroundings. He hosted sedate dinners and cocktail parties, even weddings for his closest friends' offspring in the back garden. His home was an oasis of sheer delight and old fashion, southern hospitality; a place where the absence of contemporary trappings and modern technology spoke of "old money."

It wasn't long, however, before young professionals, working in Atlanta, invaded his neighborhood, buying up the gracious old buildings and "restoring" them. To Rodney's disgust, they even knocked on his door during their excursions into the community on weekends asking if he wanted to sell his home. Although they praised him for its pristine restoration, he was outraged by their crassness, their lack of knowledge of tradition, and their offers of obscene sums of money. He refused to sell and vowed that the only way he would leave his beautiful home was to be "carried out in a box." To his profound disappointment, not a single one of his neighbors had taken his advice to restore.

Mornings, while walking his dog, Rodney fumed and cursed those nouveau riche who had moved into the grand old homes on Magnolia Street. Sold by his neighbors who could no longer afford them, or having bequeathed them to

Rosemarie Nervelle
Camden, ME

their grandchildren, the houses were renovated and redecorated with abominable taste and the cheapest materials. Shortly thereafter, they were placed back on the market at great profits. They roared in and out of the neighborhood in red Ferraris, yellow Corvettes and Harley Davidson motorcycles. Convoluted and brightly colored plastic jungle gyms and swing sets littered the beaten-down grass around the cracked aprons of the swimming pools. Children and dogs ran unrestrained through gardens surrounded by old lilac, hydrangea and magnolia trees sadly in need of attention. Garbage cans sat on the curb for days before the scheduled pick-up, and lay empty and rolling, days afterward.

Rodney had not seen them move in, nor had he yet met his new neighbors on the north side, but he already despised them. The name Bailey appeared on the garishly painted mailbox. A month before, they had purchased the old Fairfax house next door, one of the most beautiful houses on the street. Oblivious to the confusion and mess while renovations were in progress all around them, the Baileys were the partying type and entertained weekends and sometimes during the week. They obviously liked flapper-type jazz music and played it constantly at high volume. They created such late night disturbances that Rodney, reluctant to call the police, was forced to move to one of the bedrooms on the opposite side of his house. The next morning, the sun rose on Bailey's back garden and pool areas littered with bottles, dirty dishes and indefinable trash.

Trying desperately to contain his anger, Rodney wrote a tastefully worded note of complaint, included his telephone number, and pushed it through the slot in Bailey's mailbox. A week later, not having received a reply, Rodney surreptitiously checked the box. The note glowed whitely and undisturbed from within.

Between the hammering during the day and the noisy revelry at night, Rodney was at his wit's end. He kept constant watch, hoping to catch Mr. Bailey on his way in or out.

Rosemarie Nervelle
Camden, ME

The Bailey family, however, were as elusive as butterflies, driving Rodney to distraction.

One night during a thunder storm which precluded yet another party, one of Bailey's magnolia trees between the two houses was destroyed by lightening. Rodney took the event as an omen. The downed tree afforded him almost uninterrupted views of the Bailey property, allowing him to keep an eye on what he was sure were illicit activities.

On one particular night during one of his neighbor's parties, tinny strains of the Charleston wafted across the gardens. Curious, Rodney found his binoculars and looked out from an upstairs window as a dozen men and women, dressed in old-fashioned formal attire danced the Lindy. As he watched, several young people dove nude into the swimming pool. He was aghast and quickly pulled the glass from his eyes. There was a costume orgy taking place *right next door!* Drugs were probably being used, illicit sex, dirty money being laundered, only God knew what else. What to do?! Should he call the police? Telephone the Baileys and warn them to stop and desist corrupting the neighborhood? Make a citizen's arrest? He couldn't arrest them all! He sprang to his desk and with shaking hands, frantically thumbed through the pages of the telephone book.

Bagley...Baher...Bailer...Bailey...Bailey...Bailey...No Bailey on Magnolia Street. Of course, the new Bailey wouldn't appear in a telephone directory almost a year old! He must call the operator. Yes, she would have the number. He dialed and spelled the name and gave the address.

"Sorry, sir," she said sweetly. "We have no Bailey listed at that address."

"Then, what name *do* you have at that address?" Rodney shouted into the telephone.

"I'm sorry, sir. I can't give you that information.

Rodney slammed down the receiver.

"Damn it!" he hissed.

Having no other option, Rodney called the police, gave his

Rosemarie Nervelle
Camden, ME

name, address and telephone number as well as Bailey's address. He would meet them at Bailey's front door and confront the man. His jaw set with resolve, Rodney hurried across the lawn. The music blasted from the back yard and through the front door accompanied by raucous laughter. From Bailey's portico, Rodney peered impatiently down the street and saw the police car approach. *About time!*

"What seems to be the problem here, sir?" asked the police officer.

In his haste to explain everything he had seen and heard, Rodney failed to notice the music and party noise had suddenly ceased. He gestured toward the back garden and stopped, confused. He glanced toward the front window where a second ago, the lights glared and people were seen drinking and dancing.

"They probably saw the police car drive up and turned everything off. I know they're in there." Rodney banged on the door. All was silent. Rodney took the policeman's arm and led him toward the back garden. "They were swimming in the nude back here. I saw them from my upstairs window."

As they pushed open the gate, they were confronted with stacks of lumber, ladders, piles of bricks, a cement mixer and other paraphernalia of construction. The pool was bone dry, and a breeze rustled dead leaves at the bottom.

The policeman looked queerly at Rodney. "Are you sure you have the right house?"

"Don't be a fool!" Rodney snapped. "I know what I saw and what I heard."

He turned toward the back door. It stood ajar. They went inside. Rodney tripped over a tool box and swore. The policeman snapped on his flashlight. The interior of the house had been gutted; sawhorses, tools and building materials lay everywhere.

Rodney stood in the middle of the floor, dumbfounded. "I don't understand this," he said feebly.

Rosemarie Nervelle
Camden, ME

"I suggest you go back to bed, Mr. Sheppard. You might have been dreaming. It happens to people sometime. I'll write a report and send you a copy in the morning."

He saw Rodney back to his house and drove away. Rodney slowly climbed the stairs like a man sleepwalking. Surely, he couldn't have dreamed all this, but he'd rather accept the policeman's explanation than the possibility of his losing his mind. He took one last look at Bailey's dark and empty back garden, got into bed and immediately fell asleep.

A loud blast of music and sounds of laughter jarred Rodney awake. He jumped out of bed and rushed to the window. There in Bailey's garden, the nude bathers dove by twos and threes into the pool, dancers and merry makers partied even more loudly than before. Rodney pulled on his robe and slippers, ran downstairs and out his back door. When he arrived in Bailey's yard, all was quiet, dark, and undisturbed. Rodney, enraged, seized a brick from a pile and threw it through a window, then another and another. Someone yelled from a window in the house next door. He heard the police siren and two burley policemen rushed at him, wrestled him to the ground and snapped on handcuffs. Rodney, blubbering uncontrollably rode downtown in the back seat of the police car and was booked for vandalism and disturbing the peace. He spent the night in jail. His brother, an attorney, was notified and paid Rodney's fine.

An hour after Rodney's arrest, the policeman who had accompanied him earlier, pushed open the gate to Bailey's back garden. All was quiet. The property, obviously under renovation, seemed undisturbed from when he had checked it just a few hours before. In the darkness, the officer stepped on something that shattered under the heel of his boot. He shone his flashlight on what looked like a round, black dish. There was a yellow circle in the middle with barely visible print. He looked closer and silently mouthed the title from the old gramophone record: Buddy Muldoon and his Charleston Jazz Band, 1925.

Rosemarie Nervelle
Camden, ME

The officer, confounded, never reported his findings.

Rodney was never the same after his release from jail. Even his return to his beautiful home didn't seem to restore his spirits. In a few short months, his physical and mental health failed, and he died a year later of unknown cause. The house was sold.

Shortly after Rodney's death, the Bailey family, having apparently finished their renovations, moved into the old Fairfax house. Their nighttime parties continued to the distraction of the owners on the opposite side of their garden. The police were called and the same officer responded. When questioned, the homeowners' complaints were identical to those of Rodney Sheppard. The lady of the house drew the officer to a window overlooking Bailey's back garden. There were no revelers, but lounging on a chaise next to the dry swimming pool, sipping a glass of champagne, was a man who remarkably resembled Rodney Sheppard.

***

sarah p. roy
Oakland, ME

Interlude

In all things we
are not equal.
Shadows upon a white
windowsill
open to summer's rose
scented breeze.

Her grey tabby cat lies still,
waits for an opportunity.

Jean Biegun
Manitowoc, WI

Gulls in Wind

I watched eleven gulls
face a hard wind.
All stood on the sand
at sober, crisp attention.
Some would quickstep
right or left but then as quickly
realign to the keen wind.
Others preened the sand
out of their feathers
when the gusts blew less.
In rough bursts, I saw
every bird hunker Sphinx-like
facing that fierce wind.
They seemed to know readily
what to do in the difficult moments.

More gulls joined the group
to total twenty-three,
but they scattered when a lone man
on lunch break strolled near.
He moved past, and four
returned to alert position
forward to the wind.
Others landed to join them.
I could see they knew
what to do with tough times,
so I stayed in my car
in the lot at the beach
to watch them and to learn.

John T. Hagan
Springboro, OH

An Old Friend Called

An old friend called me one cold day
And left a message that did say,
"I know it's been so long awhile
Since you and I have shared a smile,
But I am now in such decline,
I'm reaching out to friends of mine.
So call me back if you'll forgive
The daily foibles that we live."
I thought about the times he had
Done things that made me truly sad.
But I said to myself at last,
"Just call him back; what's past is past."
He said he'd been hospitalized
And in that time had realized
That he no longer wished to stay
In such debilitative way.
Gangrene would now necessitate
Parts of his feet to amputate,
And he'd soon be at home alone
With only friend, a mobile phone.
I knew I should pay him a call,
And so a plan I made so small
To travel with another mate,
A visit to effectuate.
And we did go on Christmas Eve,
To both our consciences relieve,
And so relive with our sick chum
The deeds that did exceed the sum
Of youthful days here on this Earth
That filled our lives when there was dearth.
He greeted us in squalid state

(continued)

John T. Hagan
Springboro, OH

And made our negligence to hate,
For he was in such direful show
We cast our glances to and fro.
We walked o'er food-strewn floors and then
We joined him in what was his den.
The air was stale; the smell was bad,
As well as spoiling food he had.
He was nostalgic and upbeat,
So we ignored the low-set heat.
He talked of girls he'd ne'er 'gin find
And spoke at length for one he pined.
He wished to see her one more time
To tell her of her charms sublime.
And when we rose to take our leave,
He took us each by one coat sleeve
And said in pleading tone and voice,
"If you'll come back, I will rejoice."
We made our promise, safe to say,
Then went our ways for Christmas Day.
Throughout the holidays he called
To both of us, but we just stalled.
We had so many things to tend;
We had not time a heart to mend.
But when the new year took its place,
In our sad thoughts we'd see his face,
And so his house we'd often ring,
But for responses, not one thing.
And then one late-night caller told
That my old friend was found long-cold.
The phone was near him in the hall.
He had, no doubt, just tried to call
The one he thought he'd like to speak
To comfort him in time so weak.
And in first month of that new year,
At his last rites I shed a tear.

(continued)

John T. Hagan
Springboro, OH

I had been told to my dismay
My pal had died on New Year's Day.
All friends do fail us in this life,
And with each bond there will be strife,
But nothing can repair the rent
Twixt two old links like time well spent
Together in each other's care
With some old stories they can share.
I know you've heard this many ways
To call a friend, to spend some days
On any terms; it won't matter,
Long as you can laugh and chatter.
My comrade was ta'en up the aisle,
And I was glad I'd helped him smile,
But I knew there was so much more
I should have done ere he passed o'er.

***

Lou Roach
Poynette, WI

Ease

Spring water whispers over pebbles.
Shafts of sun launch a regatta
of light, ferried by the current.
Willows lean in the warming air.
Ferns glow green just above the shoreline.
I doze, back against cool bark,
lulled by long-sought solitude,
steeped in the woodland peace.

Caroline Janover
Damariscotta, ME

Circling the Drain

"We need to put your mother on a suicide watch." The supervisor at the Ebb Tide Nursing Home sounded agitated. "Your mother says she just wants to disappear. She says that staying alive is a waste of good money." There was a pause. "Your mother says she is tired of circling the drain."

I propped the phone on my shoulder, put on oven gloves and took a pan of brownies out of the oven. The kitchen smelled of warm chocolate and white hyacinths. "I'm not sure that Mom's depressed, Miss Wingate." I said sliding the brownies on the counter to cool. "Mom's a practical lady. I think she's just being realistic."

"A Resident Care Team Meeting has been scheduled for Wednesday morning," Miss Wingate replied. "Will you and your sister be attending the meeting in person or on the telephone?"

"If it doesn't snow, we'll be there," I said, turning off the oven. I was glad I'd baked brownies. My mother was addicted to chocolate.

The next Wednesday my sister Ann and I drove from mid-coast Maine to Massachusetts. When we arrived at the Ebb Tide Nursing Home, the receptionist directed us down the hall with the plush green carpet to the conference room. Mom sat in a wheelchair at the far end of the long table peering over a bouquet of red, plastic geraniums. When Ann and I walked into the room, she beamed and blew us both a kiss. Miss Wingate followed us into the conference room. She was wearing a dark-blue suit with a pink, silk scarf wrapped tightly around her neck. "Hello, Professor," she said nodding toward my mother. Mom stared at Miss Wingate, looking bewildered. "It's YOU!" she suddenly cried. That was the greeting my mother gave when she had no idea to whom she was speaking. After hugging Mom and giving her the tin of brownies, Ann and I greeted Miss Wingate and the other

Caroline Janover
Damariscotta, ME

members of the Resident Care Support Team. Mom peeked into the tin and grinned, a faint whiff of chocolate in the air. Quickly she shut the lid and hid the brownies under her plaid, wool skirt. She had no intention of sharing the brownies with anyone sitting at the table. She wanted every sweet bite for herself.

The physical therapist's report was the first on the agenda. She explained that our mother was making good progress after the fall that had broken her hip. "To walk 100 feet so soon after surgery is impressive for a 91 year old," the P/T said, gently patting Mom on the arm. Mom looked up surprised. "I broke my hip?" she asked.

"That's why you spent six weeks in the infirmary," I reminded her.

"Oh, I thought I had appendicitis. Why didn't you tell me I broke my hip?" Mom pushed a hairpin into the soft twists of white hair wrapped neatly in a bun on the top of her head. She wore pearl earrings, a pearl necklace and the diamond ring passed down through the six generations of Carolines in the family. Mom's skin was as white and wrinkled as tissue paper. Even with a dash of red lipstick smeared on her front tooth, she looked dignified.

As the dietician began to describe the eating habits of the elderly, my mind wandered to all the years I'd watched my mother sitting at the head of a table. I'd watched her teaching graduate seminars, running Child Study Team meetings and hosting elaborate dinner parties. My mother had commuted one hundred miles a day for four years to earn her PhD from Boston University. When she graduated, the School of Education immediately hired her to run the Psycho-educational Clinic. I'd just won a full scholarship to do graduate work in special education at BU and was horrified to read the name of one of my professors...Dr. Caroline Fish, my MOTHER! "Pretend we don't know each other." I pleaded. We had different last names so for a while our little incognito scheme worked. Then I noticed people looking at

Caroline Janover
Damariscotta, ME

me suspiciously. Mom had put a photo of her five children on her desk.

For the two years I was in graduate school, I watched my mother redirect and calm the most bizarre behaviors of emotionally disturbed children. She'd make her fingers into a walking, talking little bug and read hopeful futures in the palms of distraught teenagers. Mom used humor, intuition and empathy to influence countless lives. Toward the end of her professional career, she was hired by Harvard Medical School to teach moral development and Piagetian Theory to the interns. Mom put on a white coat and did rounds with the doctors. She understood the workings of the brain. When Mom's brain began to misfire, she documented her decline with almost a clinical detachment. "The hippocampus is fading today," she'd report over the phone as the mind-numbing dementia began to capture her thinking. After she retired from Harvard, Mom lived by herself year-round on Nantucket for twelve years. She made the decision to move to the Ebb Tide Nursing Home when she could no longer drive. Her greatest fear was to become a burden to her children.

After the dietician finished her report about Mom's hearty appetite, especially for desserts, the social worker cleared her throat. "Your mother is a lovely lady," she said, "but we just can't convince her to join any of the wonderful groups we have here at Ebb Tide. The Book Club, Music Appreciation Society and Art History Seminar would just love to have her join. Many of our residents enjoy Bingo Bongo and the sing-along every afternoon at 3:00 in the main lobby.

"Been there and done that," Mom muttered. "After five husbands and three children all I want is to be left alone."

"Mom, you've had three husbands and five children," Ann said softly.

"Been there, done that. I have no desire to join a group of any kind. I just want to be left alone. I want to see my family and read and write books and watch old movies on the television set."

Caroline Janover
Damariscotta, ME

"Research shows that elderly folk who engage in social activities live longer," the social worker said earnestly.

"I don't want to live longer." My mother narrowed her eyes. "As soon as I finish writing my book, I want to die. The money it costs to keep me in this place should be going toward my great-grandchildren's education." She looked at me. "Do I have great-grandchildren?"

I nodded.

Mom looked delighted, "Why didn't you tell me?" she asked.

On her 90th birthday, our mother signed her second book contract. *INTO THE WILDERNESS* was a novel based on the story of our family settling in Maine in the early 1800s. The first draft was the most confusing story I'd ever read. The main character had four different names. Mom could not remember from one chapter to the next what she'd called each character. After significant editing, her agent found a publisher. Mom was now working on a murder mystery that took place in a nursing home called *The Ebb Tide Home.*

Miss Wingate fingered through papers in a thick file. "We want people to be happy here at Ebb Tide," she said. "We are legally required to report people who are in danger of hurting themselves or others. Have you ever considered taking your life, Professor? Have you ever considered suicide?"

"Suicide! What a good idea!" Mom said cheerfully. "Will you help me? I've asked my children to bring me poison pills but they keep forgetting."

Ann kicked me under the table. Miss Wingate chewed her lip and continued, "If there is any danger..."

"What's the name of my disease?" Mom interrupted. "I can't remember the name of my disease."

"You have Alzheimer's," I said taking Mom's hand. It just means you have trouble remembering things."

Miss Wingate made a note in the file with a red pen and continued. "If your mother needs help with dressing, toileting skills or walking independently to the dining room and

Caroline Janover
Damariscotta, ME

feeding herself, she will have to be transferred to the Dementia Wing here at Ebb Tide. We run the Wing "family style." All the residents eat, socialize, sing and exercise together every day.

"What's the name of my disease?" Mom repeated.

"You have Alzheimer's Disease," Ann said reassuringly.

"I just want to disappear," Mom said, looking out the window. "What do I have to live for? I've lost my mind and I still have appendicitis. Besides, it costs a fortune to live here on Nantucket."

"There are chocolate brownies in that tin," I said pointing to the bulge under Mom's skirt. "Before you disappear, let's go eat some brownies."

Mom pushed her wheelchair away from the table. "I'm going back to my room to eat brownies with my girls," she announced. "Thank you all for coming to dinner."

Ann and I stood up and said good-bye to Miss Wingate and the Resident Care Support Team. We agreed to have a follow-up conference call in a week. When we caught up with Mom in the hallway, she was talking to a lady rocking a baby doll in her arms. "When circling, eat chocolate," Mom said in a professional tone, handing the lady a brownie. "I must remember to tell that to my students," Mom muttered as she continued to push her wheelchair down the long corridor to her small, sunny, single room.

Helen Rivas-Rose
Kennebunk, ME

Stone Monument

In a flash it's gone
A half-second dream,
A huge dark grey icon,
Hung in my dining room,
Dwarfing a painting.

A bulging stomach and angular face with
Noticeable portion missing.
I ponder still,
Easter Island fashion, what was it,
Why?

***

Alive on a Late Summer Afternoon

Above my lush meadow
Invisible to me
Mosquitoes thrive
I see dogged dragonflies cruise,
Feed, outdone only by
Frenzied, hungry swallows
Swirling, high, low, swerving, darting, diving.
And me, from my couch, pondering the finality
Of everything living.

Cindy Partington
Dallas Center, IA

Old Neighbors

in her kitchen
he shuffled across faded green linoleum
ignoring the ancient pain
favoring the leg
he'd almost lost a lifetime ago
when she'd known the right thing to do
perfect in ruffled white finery
too fragile to play
she broke loose from her mother's grip
and ran headlong and stumbling for help
while the rest stood
transfixed by his twisted flesh
he'd thanked her
properly, of course
with words and tears
but now was time
now was the season
a time to be born, a time to...
repay the debt
lifting small spoons of water
to her wrinkled lips
gently touching her thin hair
holding her bony fingers
sure her frightened eyes
had no idea
who he was

Liz Rhodebeck
Pewaukee, WI

Firstfall

I awake to leaf snow
fluttering outside my window
great golden handfuls
like birds' wings in a fairy tale,
nature's confetti of laughter
tumbling, swirling, they keep falling
a strange blizzard of color
my lungs lifted with
this helium air of autumnal delight
cheeks and eyes clear for the first time
since long ago winter.
I hurry to rush into the street
and scuff my way through
the overflowing curbs and gutters
making a sound like a tide, hissing
and swishing round my ankles
coast of a curb, waves of maples
in jubilant tones of yellow, henna, umber, dark green
walking the whole length of the street
in the gutter, drunk with the smell
of dry crisp leaves, inhale
handfuls of their earthly scent, rub
them on my cheeks, my hair and recall
my daughter, just eleven, not quite
a woman but barely still a girl, helping me
rake a pile three feet deep in
the corner of the yard;
we fell into it like a feather bed,
felt the warmth of the earth
through the leaves, imagined sleeping
there forever like pioneers or Indians,

(continued)

Liz Rhodebeck
Pewaukee, WI

her face still in wonder at what
a leaf bed could be, what life could be
the moment trembling like the
last oak leaf on the branch above us
pierced by a final arrow of autumn sun
humming in the air.
And so I stop to stuff
leaves in my pockets,
scatter them on my hardwood floors
and tabletops, to remember.

***

Earl Weigelt
Winslow, ME

One Got Away

The fly was presented high-floating and clean
with just enough upstream mend,
and it drifted the lane without a ripple,
to dark water inside the bend.
A trout's head appeared, wide across as my fist;
he sipped my caddis down deep
and bulled for the bottom with a rush and a swirl,
scorching the drag on my reel.
He ran me to backing, made me sprint down the bank
then he found a great boulder to run to,
surged a right angle, charging the shallows
clipping my tippet in two!
He lay there a minute, free as a bird
just long enough for me to eye him
then he finned for the depths as if he were weary,
disgusted a grown man was crying.

Robert Erickson
Round Pond, ME

My Grandfather in Kind

The old man sits in the rocking chair
He also sits in a young picture over there
A man of the past, yet in my mind
He lives in chairs and pictures of a kind

Rocking there with glistening eyes toward me
Telling pictured stories of how life used to be
Of hard work, sacrifice, honor and morality
Building blocks of character he wanted me to see

His bony hand takes me to his sweatered lap
Softly he cradles me for my afternoon nap
When he hums in that soothing low voice
The blanket of sleep overcomes, I have no choice

Where are you now Grandpa because I love you so
I want my head on your chest again, please don't go
You are gone but my fond memories of you will bind
As you still live in your chair and my heart in kind

Terri Parker
Richmond, ME

Chewing Surprise

Tasting the hard, thick, brown square of dark chocolate Grampie finally agreed to share with me after succumbing to ten tortuous minutes of my innocent childlike begging, my mouth explodes. My eyeballs seem pushed back into my now-aching head and I wonder where the loud buzzing sound is coming from. Not sure who is doing all the screaming. Ohhhhh noooooo, it's coming from ME!

I begin intermittently spitting into the dusty gravel driveway and yelling and spitting and yelling and spitting and yelling something indistinguishable. My legs begin to go wobbly and my arms are flailing as if I were going to take flight. I WANT to fly away! Faaaaarrrrr away from my HERO, my Grampie who is now doubled over, laughing hysterically in his deep, gravelly voice until tears roll off his rosy cheeks and his shiny bald head is as red as a boiled lobster.

The spitting and yelling continues until he can once again stand upright and pulls me to his chest with a big bear hug. Gramie, in her full-length, crisply ironed cotton apron emerges from deep within the house, most probably the kitchen, with a Tom and Jerry jelly glass of cold, red ZA-REX. She had been carefully watching out the tall kitchen window as we walked through the yard on our weekly trek to inspect the "blueberry fields" and had witnessed the entire interaction. She anticipated this very outcome as she watched my begging her playful husband and saw that he had finally handed me a chunk of his "brownie."

That moment was the first time I became aware of Grampie's lifetime love of chewing tobacco! He surely did covet chewing chunks of that nasty smelling stuff! Wherever he went, a fresh double-brownie sized chunk, newly wrapped in cellophane, rode in the breast pocket of his plaid flannel shirt. It truly seemed his special friend at times. He reached into that secret hiding place for refreshment, out of boredom,

Terri Parker
Richmond, ME

for consolation and for comfort. It seemed that chewing centered and calmed him all at the same time, just as a baby doll or soft blanket does when we are small.

It is NOT much of a stretch to imagine how I thought this enticing brown substance to be a luscious brownie. I was salivating for a chocolaty treat as I marched proudly alongside the strong, wise Grampie I adored.

None of the three of us ever forgot that awakening, my first exposure to the cognizance of chocolate versus tobacco. The recounting of that day continued for years, being told and retold from family holiday dinner tables to random visitors after I was long tucked away in bed.

He did so love to CHAW. He chewed while walking outside first thing in the fresh air of morning. He chawed a chunk after eating a hearty lunch. He chawed vigorously while driving the car and much to my embarrassment, spit the "juice" out of the driver side window. Sometimes if the window was only partially down, the juicy drool left drips that ran down the clean window glass like muddy stripes. If he chose to spit while the car was in motion, I would wait until the stripes curled at the bottom, looking to my innocent little girl mind like upside down chocolate candy canes.

When I was in my 40's and Grampie was nearing the end of his life, he lay pale and struggling for breath and dignity from a hospital bed. Unable to speak much above a whisper, he crooked his finger to draw me closer to his face and asked me to go into his closet to reach into his worn flannel shirt pocket for something for him. I was NOT surprised to feel the "chunk of CHAW" he was asking me to sneak to him.

As I crossed the room I was overwhelmed by memories of his love affair with chewing. Those memories however had FAR less an impact than the look of sheer delight I saw in his twinkling eyes as I handed him the treasure he had so longed for during his lengthy stay at the hospital. His tired, worn, scraggly face seemed to glow and his age faded away at that moment.

Terri Parker
Richmond, ME

He grabbed onto the chunk of chewing tobacco and clutched it to his chest under the crisp white hospital sheets for the remainder of our visit. He thanked me with a whisper in my ear as I hugged him for what we both knew would probably be the last time. I remembered the first time he shared his brownie with me.

At Grampie's funeral, we all passed his casket slowly, some lingering to pay a tribute in their own special way. I tucked my favorite pinky ring (a simple love knot) into the breast pocket of the shirt where he always kept his beloved chewing tobacco. As I sat on the hard wooden bench facing his casket, I watched as my sister tucked a fresh package of chewing tobacco into the very same breast pocket, her special gift for his next journey.

***

Jim Mello
Farmington, ME

No Match

the pastel pioneer crocuses
and the soft glowing
second wave daffodils

are no match
for the blood red tulips

rising in their moment
from the deep dark earth
shaking off hibernation

in screaming scarlet

Jeanine Stevens
Sacramento, CA

After a Few Years

You're in the village,
somewhere. If I wandered
small streets, I might see you,
still robust but older,
coming out of the library
in tweeds, or studying Colette
in the coffee house.
Only a glimpse.
We would meld into others,
two at the same point
checking clocks, wanting
more time, or having
too much time.
Once, we went to the shore
for lunch like so many others.
But, I wonder.
Sometimes at Redondo Pier,
I'll be eating fried prawns
like the ones we loved.
Then, walk the beach,
watch phosphorescent waves
looping in, your eyes,
liquid blue—
your face suntanned,
rimmed in solar flares,
swimming swiftly toward me.

Roger M. Woodbury
Morrill, ME

Grampa's Favorite Rock #6

She took him to the cottage that summer. They watched the gentle waves, and sat on a large flat rock. It was her grandfather's favorite rock, she told him.

"Let's swim," she said, excited. She swam strongest, dove beneath and surfaced behind him. Like a playful seal she leapt on his back and he felt her legs wrapped around him. Flailing and sputtering he surfaced. She laughed as he swam after her.

They huddled in an old beach robe, its coarseness blocking the breeze from their shivering nakedness. He kissed her. She welcomed his touch that first time. "I want us always to come here," she said.

That afternoon they swam. Their two little boys splashed and dove like playful seals. Afterward they huddled on her grandfather's favorite rock, the big beach robe blocking the stiff afternoon breeze from their wet flesh. He told them of sitting here with their mother before they were born.

Now looking toward the setting sun, he imagined her sitting on the rock. Upstairs he heard the boys' restless sleep as he looked at the picture of her smiling face and camouflage cap beside the tightly cased flag.

The inscription on the photo read: "Fallujah."

Anne Hammond
Woolwich, ME

Kyle's First Sail

My hand on the tiller holding the wind,
I fly our 40-foot bird,
Setting our island course.
The wind packs the power,

But I pick the points of sail,
A reach, to lay the beam on the sea,
A beat, to race into the source of wind,
A run, to tail off the last downward rush.

The big bird roars like an eagle soars,
Balanced, broad to the wind.
The eagle will fly as I command;
This is the challenge a sailor demands.

What dark signal comes from churning clouds?
The sky is black; the radio broken;
No warning from NOAA, no land stations far offshore.
What can I do? Read the weather as all men once did.

I am the master guiding the vessel;
I order my shipmates to trim the sails, navigate our course.
If the front won't blow through, I'll search
For a weather hole where wind can not reach.

I have the courage to deal with the trials;
The storms that arise without warning,
Hidden coral reefs under altered sunlight.
I build my own mastery;

When to trim the sail,
When to reef, where to anchor.
I know how to trust the wind;
I hold the tiller of my shipmates' lives.

Zibette Dean
Edgecomb, ME

Blessing of the Fleet

In the quiet water of the inner harbor
lobster boats process around the docks,
many boats, more than the home fleet.

They come from coves up and down the coast,
men who lie about where the catch is,
cut each other's warps,
but come quick to help in trouble.

At the dory monument, before Our Lady
Queen of Peace, clergy offer prayers.
The church bell tolls. A voice:

Thomas Lewis, 1754, lost at sea.
James Tibbetts, 1802, fell from the foremast.

The bell tolls.

Charles Campbell, 1814, lost at sea.
John and Benjamin Carter, age 14, and 17, lost on the
        Grand Banks.

The bell tolls.

The boats file past the monument,
receive the blessing of the community.

Stacy Bervig
Alamosa, CO

I Met You at the Bridge One Day

I met you at the bridge one day.
You took my hand and we laughed
from one end to the other, crossing
the waters of a wicked, brooding heart.
When we reached the other side
you let go
and jumped in.
I thought about following you
for a second,
but my thought quickly faded when I realized I was only
       jumping in to save you from a
place not savable.
I watched you drown
in a place so deep
I could scarcely watch—so I stopped.
I stood alone on the bridge,
crossed back over by myself
and glanced back only once.
Kick hard,
thrash your arms.
Learn to swim.
I'm not going to wait,
but maybe next time you won't let go.

Bill Tucker
Aurora, OH

Big I.M.

The son of Big I.M. looked at the flowers that had been arranged around the coffin. There were a great many, mostly carnations. *If they just wouldn't send so many carnations, it wouldn't smell so much like a funeral,* he thought. It would be another twenty minutes before the service started; time enough for a lot more people to come and tell the family how sorry they were about the death of Big I.M. It was very trying for all of them. The flowers offered a momentary diversion for John's thoughts, and he began to regret that the funeral had not been held out in the country as had been planned at first. At the country graveyard, there would have been all the country folk and the Negroes that had been the real actors in his father's life. Here, there were few of the rural people and none of the Negroes. As he sat and looked at the flowers and thought about the blacks and poor white farm people that had filled his father's life for the last thirty years, he remembered another funeral he had witnessed over fifteen years ago.

***

"Penn, you stop that damn dancing around and tell me what the hell you want."

The Negro was on the front porch of Bill Wilant's house, shuffling from one foot to the other, with his hat being mangled in his nervous hands.

John had heard this type of impatient challenge from his father many times. All the Negroes danced when they talked to Big I.M. It was instinctive. They knew he wouldn't let them off easy.

"Give them hell before you give them anything," he told John. "If you don't, they won't respect you."

They never paid anything back and Big I.M. didn't expect

Bill Tucker
Aurora, OH

them to. But he never turned one away hungry or cold, and it was the Negroes that had started calling him Big I.M. John never really knew when or where it had started. He had thought it might have come out of the Tennessee hill country that produced his father or from the railroad shops where Big Bill Wilant had worked for thirty-five years. Brutally hard work, from eighteen to fifty-three, before he had enough of it and bought five hundred acres of Mississippi bottom land and went back to the country.

Actually it had taken the Mississippi Negroes to find any association between a man like Bill Wilant and God. They called God *Great I.M,* or perhaps it was *Great I Am,* and they confused the white man that controlled their destinies to such a great extent with their own peculiar conception of what God should be. Bill Wilant didn't like to be confused with God, and refused to allow them to call him Big I.M. in his presence, but when he wasn't there to overhear, he was so identified. The black man before him had just called him Mister Bill; he allowed that.

When Wilant finished his half-minute tirade he said, "All right, what do you want now, and it better not be money. I gave you a dollar yesterday."

"Well, suh. When I was talkin' to Edna, she said 'Don' you know a pore nigger like you is ain't gonna—' "

"For Pete's sake, Penn! Don't tell me what your old woman said every time I ask you a question. What do you want?"

"Yassuh," Penn was almost hopping from foot to foot now, in an effort to get out what he had to say. "She said a pore nigger like I is ain't gonna git the doctuh out here since I owes him a little something anyways for the time when Noah . . . "

John sat on the back steps and listened. He was grinning broadly when his father passed him. Wilant glowered briefly at his son and then went to the back door and called his wife.

Bill Tucker
Aurora, OH

"Jenny," he called through the screened door. There was an answer from the kitchen, and he continued, "Call the doctor for Penn." He went back into the backyard and confronted Penn, "Who do you want the doctor for?"

"Cook, Mistuh Bill. He cut hisself."

Wilant started, then he walked within a foot of Penn and scowled into his face. "Penn, don't you lie to me. Who cut Cook; has he been fighting again?"

Penn's face was twisted in anguish. Cook was his son. "It wasn't no fight, Mistuh Bill. Some gal cut him last night." There was terror in the old Negroe's eyes, and John had stopped laughing, sobered by the pain in Penn's face.

"You mean Fanny don't you? Did Fanny cut him again?" Wilant demanded, searching the now inscrutable face before him.

"Nawsuh, hit wasn't Fanny. Hit was some other gal. Cut him last night at Mistuh Cassidy's." Penn's lips were tight and Wilant knew he couldn't force anything from him. It could have been any of the Negro girls in the neighborhood, made savage and vengeful from the cheap bootleg whiskey that Fred Cassidy exchanged for hard earned money on a Saturday night at his beer parlor and general store. Fanny was Cook's wife, possessive and jealous, and unknown to Penn, the spurious product of an unremembered Saturday night linking with some dead and forgotten chance acquaintance.

Jenny Wilant leaned out the back door and called to her husband, "Dr. Freeman wants to know, are we calling or is Penn calling? He wants to know what's the matter."

"Tell him you're calling for Penn. Cook got stabbed at Cassidy's last night, but don't tell him that. Tell him it's a bad cut."

Jenny disappeared into the house and then reappeared after a short time to address her husband again.

"Doctor Freeman said he couldn't come. Penn owes him some money and he says he never gets paid and ten miles is

Bill Tucker
Aurora, OH

a long way from town to come and not get paid—"

"Tell the pompous ass to get out here," Wilant exploded in sudden anger. "No, wait. I'll tell him myself." He went into the house and could be heard telling the doctor, in effect, what he had told his wife to tell him. He left out the name, but none of the violence. Calling Penn to the back door he instructed him briefly, "Go home and try to keep the rest of the niggers from killing him. The doctor will be here in thirty minutes. I'll be over there after a while."

Directed by Wilant, John gathered up some bandages and iodine and both of them set off down the road toward the shack occupied by Penn and his family, including Cook and Fanny. They walked for the most part in silence. John was almost twenty years old but still possessed a small boy feeling of hesitancy about speaking to his father in matters of great gravity. The dust along the road coated their shoes with a thin powdery film and rose in small puffs to encircle their ankles at every step. John looked out across the fields that the June rains and the July sun had made green and luxuriant. The heat rose in shimmering, almost liquid waves everywhere he looked. They turned in at the path that led to Penn's shack and Wilant looked up the small incline at the cluster of black people waiting for the climax the white man represented.

"Savages," Wilant said, "They're still savages. Give 'em half a chance and they'll kill themselves off."

John had heard him say that before. Now he wondered what his father would do, if they did. He depended on the Negroes; they were not expendable in his life. He knew that his father wouldn't be as generous to white men, that he had a depth of feeling for them that was inadequately hidden by his bluff, uncompromising exterior. He, in turn, was their deliverer and keeper, their salvation and their strength.

Reflecting on these things and realizing that his thought patterns were taking the form of a circuit riding preacher's biblical cliches, he became inwardly amused and was smil-

Bill Tucker
Aurora, OH

ing to himself when they came up to the treacherously inse-
cure looking front porch of the shack. Wilant had brushed
past the Negroes, standing with sober faces and studied atti-
tudes of great despair, and gone inside. John followed with
the bandages and iodine.

Cook was unconscious; his breath gurgled in his throat,
liquid sounding and sporadic. Wilant stood glowering down
on the long frame of the thirty-year-old black man, naked
except for an incredibly clean pair of white socks. For all his
blackness, Cook seemed wan and wasted. Penn lifted two
pads of folded sheets, bandages that were hardly stained,
exposing the unfatal looking pink-white wounds in the belly
and chest. John was relieved. The openings in the flesh
seemed harmless in their neat and un-bloody pinkness.

Wilant stood without comment for some time, studying
the wounds, thinking that perhaps he shouldn't have wast-
ed the time necessary to make Penn respect him. He should
have known from the trouble in Penn's eyes. But then he
realized that it wouldn't have made any difference. In his
mind and to himself he said, *They waited over twelve hours
to be sure he was done for, crouching around him, protective,
exclusive, waiting to be sure before they called in the white
man.*

"There's not a pint of blood left in him," Wilant spoke
aloud. But it was almost inaudible, as if to himself again, a
musing studied thought. Penn looked at Big I.M. knowing
what he had said, understanding what it meant, accepting it.
He put the bandages back in place and followed the two
white men to the door of the shanty. Penn's wife, Edna,
could be heard shuffling around to the side of the bed as they
left. Mournfully, she started to call upon Great I.M. as they
went into the yard.

"Where's Fanny, Penn?" Wilant asked mildly, inquisitive-
ly, as they came out into the sunlight and breathed the dark-
ness out of their lungs.

"She's in dare, Mistuh Bill, sittin' by the stove in the

Bill Tucker
Aurora, OH

kitchen," Penn pointed back toward the shack. "I thought you seed her."

Wilant looked into the inscrutable face before him knowing the futility of more questioning. He turned to the group of Negroes that had moved from the front porch when he arrived and stood now by the side of the shack. Of the seven or eight there, all but two were his farm hands. The other two were from a neighboring farm.

"Jess, did any of you see who stabbed Cook?"

"Nawsuh, Mistuh Bill, I ain't seed nobody stab him. I wasn't dare," Jess answered. His face was troubled and it was plain that he hoped Wilant wouldn't question him further. Wilant thought of asking him where it was that he hadn't been, bur realized it would be useless. He examined the rest of the black, enigmatic faces. They were almost sullen in anticipation of an inquest personally conducted by Wilant. Standing by his father, John seemed to be reading his thoughts, knowing there would be no more questioning, feeling, as Wilant felt, the unfathomable kinship of these people who protected their own, guilty and innocent alike.

"Stay out of the house and leave them alone," Wilant said and John knew that they would stay out by the way he had said it, not demandingly but without even the consideration in his voice that they could do otherwise but obey him.

The sun was a little higher and there was no wind. John shaded his eyes as he walked, seeing nothing but the gravel in the road directly in front of him. A shapeless straw hat protected the eyes of Wilant, and he stared straight down the road toward the house.

"What do you think?" John asked his father without looking up or removing the shading hand from his eyes. Wilant didn't answer but walked on deliberately, as if he hadn't heard. For several minutes the only sound was the crunch of the gravel under their feet. Finally, John peered from under his hand at his father and spoke again, "It didn't seem so bad to me." He was remembering the inoffensive pink

Bill Tucker
Aurora, OH

flesh of the unmortal seeming wounds. John had not seen much of death or its prelude.

Wilant looked at John and then returned to his scrutiny of the road before him. "Cook will be dead within an hour," he said, as if he were impatient with John for not recognizing what he had seen.

John stopped still in the road, his bottom jaw swung down in open-mouthed disbelief. Wilant strode on ahead without slowing or looking back. "Dead!" John exclaimed. "But he looked—the cuts didn't seem—Hell! He looked in pretty good shape to me." He was shouting now at his father's retreating back. In an hour, Cook would be dead—he had said it, so it was true. No shouting or reasoning, or thinking about how the wounds looked, not even a white doctor could change it. Indestructible, ageless Cook, who was thirty years old and had looked thirty years old ever since he could remember and who would have looked thirty years old forever, would be dead in an hour. John looked across the fence into the corn field—corn growing out of soil that Cook had taught him to plow when he was seven years old. Beyond the cornfield a froth of dark green treetops shaded the river. He remembered carrying the jar of grasshoppers that Cook forbid him to drop and the slaughter pole that he dragged along, holding onto the big end. That was when he was only five, the first time he saw the river.

When he caught up to Wilant they were almost home. Nothing was said until they turned into the front yard and then John spoke. "What're you going to do about Fanny?"

"Nothing. That's a job for the sheriff, and he won't do anything either," Wilant said.

"Why not? You know she did it."

"Yes, I know it, and you know it, and all the niggers know it, but the sheriff doesn't know it, and he's too damn dumb to find out. They'll send him on a couple of wild goose chases after some niggers that don't exist, and they might even haul a couple of them into town, but nobody will say they

Bill Tucker
Aurora, OH

saw anything. Fred Cassidy didn't see it. He never has seen anything happen in that butcher shop of his. The sheriff won't try too hard anyway and I guess it's just as well. Nobody cares if niggers kill each other; they just don't want them to steal anything." He contemplated his son's face as he spoke, wondering if he understood that taking Fanny into town and having the white men hang her wouldn't solve anything. "Are you going to tell them she did it?" he asked finally.

John seemed to grasp what he meant and looked meditatively at the ground for a few moments. "No, I didn't see her do it," he said.

While Wilant was talking on the telephone, the doctor roared past the house in his new 1938 Ford V-8, sending a wake of dust into the air to settle onto the already brown vegetation at the roadside. When he came back twenty minutes later Wilant and John were back out in front of the house waiting for him. Freeman was over fifty and carried two hundred pounds on his short frame, so he strained and grunted in the act of getting from behind the wheel and onto the ground. He walked fatly up to the Wilants.

"Hello, Mr. Bill." He nodded to John and mopped his face with his handkerchief before he spoke again. "You should have called an undertaker instead of a doctor." He laughed at the joke he had made.

"Was Cook dead when you got there?" Wilant asked.

"Not quite. I finished him off, I guess." He chuckled again at his humor. "What happened? He get in a fight again, or was it a woman?" Freeman knew the Negroes from other trips he had made. In town he called them savages because he had heard Wilant call them that once. The things they did made entertaining stories for him to tell to the men in the Rotary Club.

"I don't know. Can't get anything out of them," Wilant said.

John wondered if he should mention anything about

Bill Tucker
Aurora, OH

Fanny. He decided against it.

"Maybe you better call the sheriff when you get back to town so he can come on out here and do what fooling around he's going to do. I want to get Cook buried tomorrow. They'll keep him out of the ground a week if nobody buries him for them," Wilant said.

"Okay. I'll get him to come on out here. Cook died while I was there, so I can act as coroner as far as he's concerned. You plan on getting him buried tomorrow. Since he's off your place I guess Haverty will come by and ask you if you know anything about it, who might have done it, I mean. I'll tell him to come here first so you can be through with it." Haverty was the sheriff and Wilant agreed that the sooner he talked with him the sooner he could get on with the business of getting Cook buried.

"How much did Penn owe you for coming out to see Noah?" Wilant asked.

Freeman considered a moment and then answered, "He still owes me two dollars."

"Here," Wilant held out a five dollar bill. "This should straighten him out with you."

"Thanks," Freeman said and pocketed the bill. He wondered if the Negroes ever paid back anything but didn't voice his thoughts. "Well, I'd better get back into town. Sorry there was nothing I could do."

The Wilants watched him until he disappeared down the road in a cloud of dust, then they turned and went into the house.

Wilant cranked the handle on the side of the telephone box and muttered inventive curses while he waited impatiently for the country operator to answer. Finally he shouted a number into the mouthpiece and listened to the far away ring above the irritating hum of the rural line.

John sprawled into one of the wicker chairs in the living room and watched his father. One leg made an impatient arc as it bounced up and down over the chair arm. He listened

Bill Tucker
Aurora, OH

as Wilant started talking into the telephone and registered surprise when the first sentence uttered was a request for the price of a casket. The other end of the line must have been surprised, too, and his father had to explain that nobody in the family had died, just one of the farm hands. There was some conversation about the welfare department and finally his father bellowed into the phone, "Did you ever try to get any charity on Sunday?" After that everything that was said had to do with the casket. His father became angry once more, apparently over a price that was mentioned. Finally, he shouted that sixty-five dollars was what the party on the other end of the line would get and to be damn well sure the casket was delivered by ten o'clock the next morning. Then he hung up. John didn't say anything, but his face held the question as he looked up at his father.

Wilant leaned against the wall in silence, still holding on to the telephone receiver. After some seconds he scowled and almost spoke, but then he turned and walked out into the front yard. Before John decided to follow him, Wilant came back in the front door. He must have thought he owed his son some explanation because he said, "Cook worked for me for fifteen years and I'm not going to bury him in a pine box."

Phillip Haverty, the sheriff, came to Wilant's door about four o'clock in the afternoon and knocked. Wilant met him there and told him in forty-five seconds what he knew factually about Cook's death. He didn't mention Fanny. That wasn't one of the known facts. The sheriff was not invited inside the house and Wilant talked through the screen door. Haverty made several comments about Negroes stabbing each other and asked a few useless questions. Then he left. The interview lasted less than five minutes.

The sheriff went back to town with three suspects, all male and all black. They were back on the farm before dark and Penn made them honorary pallbearers to show his gratitude and his appreciation of their forbearance.

Bill Tucker
Aurora, OH

The casket came at nine o'clock the next morning. John went out to the road in front of the house and looked at it. It was covered with brown upholstery material and had six fake brass handles for the pallbearers. Before he could look inside, Wilant told the driver of the funeral-home truck to take it on down to Penn's shack and then Wilant got in and went with him. As he watched the truck sink in the cloud of dust from its own wheels, John thought of the casket and the finality of Cook's life it represented. He thought of the sixty-five dollars, that was two month's wages for a farm hand, and knew that there were pine boards under the brown upholstery. For some reason he remembered his father shouting into the telephone mouthpiece, "Did you ever try to get any charity on Sunday?"

At five in the afternoon the handles on the casket were too hot to touch. It had been out in the sun for almost eight hours in back of Penn's shack because none of the doors were wide enough to accommodate it. A murmuring vanguard of admiring blacks had felt and inspected it, alternately standing, squatting, examining it untiringly.

John drove Wilant's pickup truck to Penn's shack and stopped by the casket. Jenny Wilant was in the front seat with him. At four-thirty, Wilant had peremptorily dismissed the casket watchers, and Cook had been placed inside. Now everything was ready.

"Put it in the truck," Wilant said.

Six men scrambled for the handles and strained it into the truck bed. The handles burned in their calloused hands.

Wilant went into the shack and emerged with Penn, Edna, and Fanny in front of him. He directed them to get into the truck with the casket.

"All right, you pallbearers get in on the other side. The rest of you will have to walk," Wilant said.

The truck with "Wilant's Dairy" lettered on each door and carrying three white people in the front seat and nine Negroes and an occupied casket in the back started toward

Bill Tucker
Aurora, OH

the country burial grounds a mile away. As the walking procession started, an enormous black woman said to her walking companion, "Ain't nobody but Fanny stabbed Cook."

The truck arrived twenty minutes before the others and the casket was lifted from the truck and placed on ropes by a freshly dug grave. The shadows were long, and the casket was in the shade, so the Negroes stood about it furtively peering into the hole in the red clay.

"Who's going to do the reading?" John asked, nodding toward the Bible, Jenny Wilant held in both hands pressed to her chest.

"I am," Wilant said. John noticed several pieces of paper protruding from between the leaves of the Book, markers. He had never seen his father read the Bible and wondered what he had selected. *Oh, my,* John thought, *he hasn't been inside a church since I've been born and he's going to conduct a funeral; undertaker and preacher, Big I.M.'s personally burying one of his own.* I'm surprised he didn't dig the grave. Maybe he did dig it. If he didn't, he watched to see that it was dug right.

"Our Father, Who art in heaven," Wilant began to recite the Lord's Prayer. He had arranged the pallbearers and the family where he wanted them after the others arrived and the prayer signaled the beginning of Cook's burial ceremony. "Hallowed be Thy name." He continued in a voice that rang powerfully in the stillness of the afternoon. He recited perfectly until the final   "Amen." After that he read the Twenty-third Psalm and after that the One Hundred and Seventh. John failed to see any great relevance in the latter selection and rather suspected it had been chosen because of its length and his father's desire to make the ceremony respectably long. With a great deal of feeling Wilant recited "Invictus" emphasizing the last two lines in such a manner as to be paradoxically out of keeping with any of the preceding importunities on Cook's behalf. When he had finished this last recitation, he motioned for the pallbearers to begin

Bill Tucker
Aurora, OH

lowering the casket. As it was lowered he said, "Dust thou art to dust returneth was not spoken of the soul."

***

It was hard for John to say anything to the old railroad men who came over and took his hand and painfully wrung out the inept phrases of sympathy.

"He was a great old man, son. Bill Wilant damn near killed me, but he made a man out of me," one sixty-five year old man said. He had served his apprenticeship under Big Bill and had worked hard for it. The old man started to go, looking not at John anymore but at a scene over thirty years past. "I've seen him break a man, too. Not really. . ." he checked himself and then added, "I'm real sorry, son." He walked over and sat down.

It was a relief when the preacher started the service that was to be held at the funeral home. When the casket was closed, John had a few bad moments but managed not to cry. He concentrated on the purely physical problem of getting into the car and being driven to the cemetery and diverted his thoughts to the extent that he was more self-possessed when the car pulled up to the cemetery plot than he had been all afternoon.

John didn't cry at all during the graveside service, and as the casket was lowered into the earth, he stood and watched it until it rested on the floor of the grave. He looked up and stared vacantly across the cemetery toward the road leading back out into the country and the domain of Big I.M. As he looked, something seemed to be demanding his attention, and he realized that a lone figure was standing by the fence on the far side of the cemetery, some hundred yards away.

He recognized Penn, standing with his hat in his hand in much the same attitude he remembered from years gone by. John stood for what seemed to everyone at the graveside a

Bill Tucker
Aurora, OH

very long time as he looked at Penn. Mentally he was calcu-
lating how long it had taken this eighty-year-old Negro to
walk the ten miles into town so that he could stand on the
outside of a white man's fence and watch Big I.M. be buried.

Abruptly John broke from his reverie, and, stooping
down, he picked up a handful of damp Mississippi clay. As
he let it rattle onto the casket, he suddenly remembered and
began, "Dust thou art . . ."

***

Zibette Dean
Edgecomb, ME

Schooner's Hull
After the painting by Edward Hopper

Her old gray bones are laid
against a concrete wall
under bleak autumn sky.

Did she carry lime from the quarries,
coal for Rockland's kitchens,
cans of sardines?

The sea where she worked is not seen.
Walls of a block of buildings
are behind her dock: a flash of sun

touches windows and chimneys.
No sign of people here. The town
has turned its back on her.

Goose River Anthology, 2012//90

Liz Moser
Baltimore, MD

Recovery

Afterwards
from being told I carried
a malignancy
that might already have
attacked me fatally

afterwards
when doctors' scalpels cut away
the tumor, leaving no disease
to feed the cancer, told me
go about your life

I wake up drained and grateful,
mystified at why I have
persistence and desire
to breathe, smile
and interact again.

My journey in a gray boat
through unknown tides and currents
is slid to shore. I am a shadow
till I absorb what once
was commonplace with sharper eyes
and newly deepened breath.

Kate Leigh
Portsmouth, NH

Star Loft

Look from Star Loft over the brim
Of island to east, of thick rock to thin
Fog, of heavy sea to light gull, of
Sweet rose to salt spray.
Amidst it all, alone, away,

A moon, a star, a seed, a pod,
A place of escape, a simple nod
To a humble mood, the rush of wings,
Inside, the lift of levels of flight,
The blink of other worldly light.

The staving off of human sound, the odd,
Drone of pulsed, silence-softened blood.

***

On the Beach

The birds sing in the rose hedges.
The sun shines high in the sky.
The fullness of salt air surrounds us.
On the soft white sand we lie.

Our skin's turned the color of mocha.
With her supple form we've merged.
No thing like a swim in the ocean.
No word like the song of a bird.

Danielle Bannister
Searsmont, ME

Default

Anger was her default setting, and Gerald was about to *willingly* switch it to "completely pissed off."

Sauntering into his mother's office he noticed her eyes pinched together in consternation. Her thin, red, lips pressed together in an ever-present hard and firm scowl. She appeared to be pissed at someone or something, undoubtedly for some trivial and asinine thing. His mother could be vicious and unforgiving in her demand for perfection; a trait which was ideal for her job, but one that proved disastrous in a human being.

"Might I have a word, Mother?" Gerald asked, trying to keep up his cheery disposition in spite of his mother's constant somber one.

"You're early," she replied without even bothering to look up from her keyboard. Gerald couldn't help but laugh at the irony.

"At least I show up," he snapped.

He leaned back against the door frame casually, waiting for her to absorb the insult. It started in her eyes first; the pinch in her eyebrows softened for a split second, seemingly bemused at her son's gall, then, just as quickly, they snapped back to attention.

Painstakingly slow, she raised her head revealing her dark eyes hovering just above the rim of her blood-red glasses.

"Gerald, please don't talk in riddles," she replied, still frantically clicking away.

Undeterred, Gerald waltzed over to the chair directly in front of his mother and plopped down. Unbuttoning his jacket and loosening his tie, he leaned in a bit, eager to wipe off her smug expression when she, predictably, thwarted his attempt.

"I presume you're upset about my missing Gwendolyn's

Danielle Bannister
Searsmont, ME

birthday party yesterday afternoon?"

Gerald bit back his anger.

"So, you did know your only granddaughter's birthday was yesterday and you still chose not to attend."

Her fingers stopped their assault on the keyboard. She turned her attention back to him, the dark circles under her eyes made her look older than she was.

"I completely understand," Gerald said, "five year olds can be quite grating on one's nerves."

It was amazing how quickly his mother could infuriate him even now, as a grown man.

"Now, Gerald, don't get so melodramatic."

"Why?" he hissed, looking at the angora rug instead of her. She didn't know how much her not being there had upset Gwen. "Why couldn't you make it? What possibly could have been more important yesterday afternoon?"

She exhaled slowly, removed her glasses and folded them carefully and placed them on top of her now closed laptop.

"I had a prior engagement," she said as though that should settle the matter.

"You had a prior engagement?"

"Yes, Gerald, that's what I said. I did telephone your home to alert you of my absence, but no one bothered to take the time to answer my call." She blinked at her son. "Now, if you don't mind, I'd like to finish what I was working on." Picking her glasses back up, she opened her laptop and, intentionally or not, shut him out.

"You are a hateful and abominable shell of a person who does not deserve the adoration Gwen bestows upon you."

His mother looked up at him, opened her mouth as though to speak, but then closed it.

Not waiting for her reply, Gerald stormed out of the office and left her alone with only the dull glow from her computer screen. Righting her posture, she looked back to what she had written. Her index finger hovered just over the delete button, but it was too late. Her mind had been made up. She

Danielle Bannister
Searsmont, ME

printed the note instead.

Without remorse, she opened her bottom drawer and retrieved the bullets she had purchased yesterday afternoon and placed them inside the handgun she had stolen from her husband early this morning. Then she walked over to the printer, folded her final note to Gwendolyn and tucked it gingerly in an envelope. Atop the envelope she wrote:

To my dearest Gwendolyn, the only one who ever truly loved who I turned out to be."

Placing the envelope next to her Last Will & Testament, she checked off her final piece of business.

***

Sherry Ballou Hanson
Brunswick, ME

Good Time

I can still get in my car,
drive to the sea, sit and watch
mica-studded ledges winking at me
in the sun, trace the rocking channel buoys
leading river to sea, watch them dazzle
on the water.

See gulls soar, hear their cries,
watch seals surfacing, their soft dark eyes
speaking their language, feel winter wind
at my back, sun on my face,
see the man with his dog
couple with a child, feel the slow
steady beating of my heart.

I can still.

Sally Belenardo
Branford, CT

Nor'easters

Beneath two heavy blankets
and knitted afghan, white and textured
as a snowdrift tracked by sparrows
under branches shedding snow, I lie,
wanting to stay where I am
and anxious to see how much more snow

all through the night, again,
covered up the shoulders of the road
and turned out lights along the coast.
Wanting to stay where I am, I know
shingles blown from roofs, boughs of oak and pine,
hedges that the snowplows broke

are deeper buried now.
Reluctant to move, I get up, look outside,
and realize I should be thankful,
for, uprooted by the first storm,
the landmark spruce tree cannot rise
from what, in other seasons, is a lawn.

Jeffrey Cannon
Worcester, MA

clean edges

Clean edges on the slides pathology surveys after
her excision surgery
Supply enough evidence that the place is clean
Hope fuels the energy for her to heal and
Pick up the habits of her life
All those things she needs and wants to do
As mother and as wife

***

her oncologist

With fatherly care he speaks to her
Of patience, strength, and hope

Aware of the challenge
He walks with her
As counselor and guide

Open to her fears
Perceptive about the limits of promises

Recognizing the value of each moment and
What gift could be there for her to cherish

*"clean edges" and "her oncologist" first published in
intimate witness: The Carol Poems by Jeff Cannon,
Goose River Press, 2004.

Jeffrey Cannon
Worcester, MA

in the shadow

She lives in the shadow of melanoma and its cures
And we along with her stumble in the dark to find our way
She holds the tender hearts of our daughters
Whose eyes look to her for answers and the safety
That allows them to sleep peacefully at night
And go about their school and play by day
To protect them for now from
What creeps on the vulnerable fringes
Of their precious lives

*"in the shadow" first published in *intimate witness:
The Carol Poems by Jeff Cannon, **Goose River Press**, 2004.

***

P. C. Moorehead
North Lake, WI

Dawning

Dawn of my day: me.
Dawn of your day: you.
Dawn of our day: child.

Marilyn Weymouth Seguin
Cuyahoga Falls, OH

Dog Days

The beauty of doing nothing is the goal of all your work, the final accomplishment for which you are most highly congratulated. The more exquisitely and delightfully you can do nothing, the higher your life's achievement. You don't necessarily need to be rich in order to experience this, either.

—Elizabeth Gilbert

The period of time between July and September when the really hot, sultry weather occurs is known as the "dog days." It is a lazy time, and the heat makes the cicadas buzz in the trees behind my camp on Little Sebago Lake in Maine. The intense heat usually coincides with high humidity. People in Maine often describe the dog days as "muggy," meaning very uncomfortable. But the dog days are my favorite time of the summer—remember, I can always cool off in the lake.

This period of time gets its name from Sirius, the "dog star" which rises and sets with the sun in the summer. The ancients believed that Sirius's heat added to that of the sun was what caused the hot weather.

The dictionary defines "dog days" a second way—as a time of inactivity, a time of doing nothing. I like this definition and during the hottest of summer days at camp, I try to take some time to be unproductive, to let life go on empty of intention—even for twenty minutes. It provides much freedom and space. None of us has as much time as we think.

But those of us who live on the lake during the summer know that the hotter the weather, the more active the lake. People from town flock to the lake with boats and jet skis to cool off in the evenings after work. And those of us who are lucky enough to live on the lake soak in its cooling waters floating on air mattresses. The children cannonball off the end of the dock until they get tired and throw sticks or balls for the dogs to retrieve. Almost everyone on my road has a dog, and although there are leash laws, most of the dogs run

Marilyn Weymouth Seguin
Cuyahoga Falls, OH

free.

My own dog Oliver loves to be at camp. One reason is that he has my undivided attention. I don't get up and leave for work every morning, and because I'm at camp, I don't go away on long business trips or vacations. I confess that all the dogs we have owned have been allowed to sleep on the furniture, and at night, slumber along beside us in the bed. Oliver sleeps attached to me like a tick. He doesn't bother me much except for the occasional leg twitching during chipmunk chasing episodes during his REM sleep. At camp, it truly is a dog's life.

Oliver is an old dog. He's lost a few teeth. When we used to strike out for Maine in the family car, Oliver would leave the driveway with his head out the window and his ears flapping in the wind. Now he has to be tranquilized. Something about the long car rides makes him nervous. He used to bark happily when I had been gone and returned. Now, he can't hear me when I come home so it might be ten or fifteen minutes before he realizes I'm there, but then he barks happily, just like always. Oliver still likes to play "throw toy" after dinner. He enjoys the company of children and other dogs. He loves to swim in the lake and ride in the kayak. He still has a puppy inside him.

Although his eyes are cloudy, he can still see anyone who approaches the camp by land or by water. Oliver is still a great watchdog, but he's easily startled when anyone approaches him from behind. I can leave the room and he doesn't realize I'm gone. Sometimes his hips hurt and his legs fail him after he's been sleeping for a long time, and he has a hard time climbing the stairs. He no longer chases chipmunks, but he insists on a morning walk. We walk the same distance as always, but we do it much more slowly than we did, say, five years ago. One day, my sister watched as Oliver struggled up the forty-two steps from the camp to our driveway, eager for his morning walk.

"Do you think you'll get another puppy one day?" she

Marilyn Weymouth Seguin
Cuyahoga Falls, OH

asked, leaving unsaid the unspeakable. My sister is a cat person. She's never had a dog. She thinks dogs demand too much attention, and that is accurate from a cat person's perspective.

"I never want to be without a dog," I reply.

When Oliver's time comes, perhaps I'll adopt an older dog rather than get a new puppy. There are advantages to adopting a mature dog. Older dogs don't generally chew up things and they are house trained. They know what "no" means. They are more calm and laid back than puppies. There is even a website devoted to the joys of owning senior dogs: It's tagline reads, "Blessed is the person who has earned the love of an old dog." Even old dogs have a puppy inside them, right?

I once wrote a book about dogs, called *The Dogs of War*. It is a collection of stories about the role of companion animals, mostly dogs, during the American Civil War, spin off research from a historical novel I was writing at the same time. Oliver was by my side as I was writing both of these books, listening as I tried out my stories on him. I talk out loud when I write, and then I type what I say—it sounds strange, but it works for me.

Oliver has heard many of my stories over the last 14 years. I imagine if he could tell me a story, he would tell me about a woman who spends her summers in Maine with a wonderful dog.

"Is that all?" I ask.

"Isn't that enough?" he replies.

Peggy Gannon
Palmyra, ME

The Pit (after September 11, 2001)

> *Grief is a hole you walk around in the daytime*
> *and at night you fall into it.*
>
> —Denise Levertov

Tonight on the summit of Goosepecker Ridge
I lay under the curve of sky
and stared between the wash of stars
into the limitless space beyond.
It was a shared communion
of laughter, wine and cigarettes
with good friends. It was as if
nothing had changed.

Only on the long ride home
I saw my essential humanity
fragile as eggshells,
saw the peace of a thousand thousand jeweled nights
shattered,
saw the shadow landscape of the future,
saw the end of laughter, heard the
silence.
I reached for the words that used to give release:
my fingers scrabbled in the empty box,
touched broken pieces, jagged edges, fractured shards of
        consonants.
I thought there was no grief so deep that language couldn't
        find it
but I've been wrong before.
I stumbled through my kitchen door
and fell into the pit.

Kimberly K. Thompson
Fairmont, WV

Erin's Lament

Slow, haunting melody
tugs at my soul, played by reed.
Wistful era, time elapsed,
rues of old, some forgotten past.
Brought to life again—renewed,
by her lovely Irish tune.
Another's land, another's sea,
another's thoughts, another's breed.
Opens my heart to Erin's woes
that wails from the piper's blow.
Oh, Erin with your forlorn past,
fair green isle of hardships lap.
Sweet tunes sung by an Irish lass,
puts my hand to heart and clasps,
as tears fall down my cheeks,
like molten glass.

***

Lou Roach
Poynette, WI

Only Then

Though skin may thin and flesh lose tone,
muscles knot and bones may splinter,
the strength of sinews, a sturdy spirit
and an open heart will withstand
more duress than we know—
until tested by the years,
we learn by surviving.

Jeannie E. Roberts
Chippewa Falls, WI

Art Fair
Near the Shores

Down Great River Road,
past the family cottage
and clear-cut memories
of lighthearted days,

a train whistle blasts
and Saturday shines
as only the third

Saturday in July can.
At Stockholm's Village
Park, artists, musicians

and fair-goers merge,
fuse with the unity
of gathering, lighten
with the poetry of place.

Stephanie Tehan Patterson
Lanark, IL

Journeys of the Lost and Found

The fog was rolling in over the water and brought with it an eeriness as my surroundings became increasingly dim. A red glow of a stoplight suddenly appeared out of the darkness. I slammed on my brakes and skidded to a halt. A figure appeared out of the haze, as if from nowhere, and as I got closer, I saw his face. It was that of an old man. The sad and weary expression painted a portrait of how life must have treated him. He staggered along in the dark with a rickety cart that housed all of his lowly possessions. His unkempt appearance and homelessness impacted me in a surprising way. In our world of plenty, I wondered how someone could become homeless. There was something that frightened me about this man.

Was it because he was a reminder of the kind of person I never wanted to become—or was I afraid of the unknown?

As I peered through my window, he unexpectedly turned his gaze toward me. There was an intensity in his look and a deep longing for days gone by—days when maybe he was the one watching the struggles of another—wanting to get away and glad it was not *him* in that situation. But now—it was.

As he made his way closer to my car, his eyes appeared to be communicating something. He was reaching out to me in some way. I quickly looked away and hoped for the light to turn green. I wanted to put this sight behind me, because it stirred something within that I did not like.

But the light stayed red. As the man reached my car, he leaned down and peered inside. He laid his hand on my window in some kind of gesture, as if he was saying hello—or maybe goodbye to a friend.

What was he trying to tell me?

This man's life was contrary to everything I had strived to achieve in my own. Here I was sitting in my high-end car,

Stephanie Tehan Patterson
Lanark, IL

wearing the latest fashions, and living in a beautiful home. People would say that I had it all. I never thought about where my next meal would come from, or if I would go hungry...again...like this man. Yet what I took for granted, he was begging for. He had nothing but a cartful of memories. His meals were leftover trash tossed out by those of us that had our fill—and yet he was probably glad to have *that*.

After what seemed an eternity, the light turned green. As the old man stepped away from my car, he never took his eyes off me. I quickly sped away. He continued to stare at me as our distance widened. His face stayed with me. I could not leave it behind...nor the feelings it evoked. I glanced in my rearview mirror one last time, as the sight of this lonely man faded. I could not shake the uneasiness within.

Was it because I found it so easy to turn my back on someone in need?

The fog grew thicker as I headed for home, and I had to fight to stay awake. I was weary from the flight and from traveling to three different states in the course of one week. I wanted to get home before the kids went to bed. My husband called me earlier and informed me that his meeting would be running late tonight, so I felt bad that the kids were home alone...again. They seemed to be growing up so quickly. My son was turning fourteen already next month, and my daughter was eleven...going on twenty. Relief flooded in as I pulled in the driveway. I was thankful to be home safely. As I pulled my bags out of the trunk, I was hoping to see the kids come dashing out to greet me—but they did not. They were always so excited to see me when they were little. Maybe they still were, but just didn't want to make it too obvious. I sure missed them. When I walked in, there they were in front of the TV. They turned and gave me a wave and the usual *Hi, Mom.* I went over to give them a hug, and they barely took their eyes off the TV. I felt a stab of pain at their indifference. I was too tired to discuss it now, so I headed up

Stephanie Tehan Patterson
Lanark, IL

to bed and decided I would talk to them about it later.

I had an early morning meeting the following day, so I didn't get a chance to see the kids. I left my usual note of instructions as I rushed out the door. When I arrived at the office, I was informed that my secretary had become ill and would be out for awhile, so the company hired me a temporary. I was not happy about that, because now I would have to take time to train someone new. As if I had the time for that. As I was leaving the meeting, one of the secretaries tracked me down and asked me if I knew about Darla, my secretary. I really did not know. She informed me that Darla had been sick with cancer and the treatments were not going well.

Darla has cancer?? I didn't even know she was sick! How could I have not known?

Hearing that Darla was sick seemed too surreal. I had just talked to her, and she seemed fine. I was torn as I thought about how badly I wanted to see her in the hospital...and the fact that I hadn't seen my kids in over a week. I decided that, for once, I would take off early so that I could do both. As I walked into her room, tears welled up within. She did not even look like herself. She was swollen and had a difficult time speaking.

How could she have gotten this sick so quickly?

When she saw me, she began to apologize for the inconvenience she was causing me. She was thinking about *me* when she was in the midst of battling this devastating disease! I quickly moved to her side and grabbed her hand and held it tight. This beautiful woman was fighting for her life. She told me how she had to confront her fears daily as she thought about what tomorrow would bring. Would she feel worse than today, or would there even be a tomorrow? I had no words to say. I didn't even begin to know how to comfort her. All I could do was be there for her and let her know how much I cared. As I went to leave, I gave her a hug and told her I would be back the following day. I was hoping nothing

Stephanie Tehan Patterson
Lanark, IL

would come up at work to keep that from happening.

As I walked out to my car, I was overcome with emotions that I could not hold back. She has been my faithful secretary for eight years, and I considered her my friend. She was always there for me, so I took it for granted that she would always be there. I began to wonder if she even knew how much she meant to me. I needed to let her know how important she was to me.

Why hadn't she told me that she was sick? More importantly, why hadn't I noticed that she wasn't feeling well?

As I drove away, a heaviness came over me. It broke my heart to see my secretary...my friend...so ill. I sat in my car and began to pray for her. I prayed that God would heal her and comfort her, because I didn't know how to.

When I got home, I hugged the kids until they said I was squishing the air out of them. I was glad to be home with them. I decided to forego writing my speech for the meeting tomorrow and spend some time with them. My husband came home early that night, so we all played games on the Wii and then just sat and talked. We hadn't talked together in a very long time. I didn't know until tonight that my son was having struggles with some bullies at school. He said they made fun of him and frequently shoved him around in the lunchroom until his tray of food went flying. He oftentimes went hungry, because his food was splattered all over the floor. My heart felt broken for the second time today.

How could anyone make fun of my beautiful son? He was so gifted, and he genuinely cared about others. He was the kind of kid that always looked out for the other guy and had their best interest at heart.

Why wasn't he being treated the same in return?

We stayed up late that night and broke the bedtime rules. When I stopped in my son's room to say goodnight, he hugged me and told me how glad he was that I was home. He told me that he missed seeing me, because I was always gone—and he added that even when I was home, I wasn't

Stephanie Tehan Patterson
Lanark, IL

really there. I was usually involved in some project for work.

I went to bed that night with a heavy heart.

Was I so caught up in my own world that I didn't even know what was going on in the lives of those I loved? How could I have let this happen?

Instantly I had a flashback of the homeless man I encountered the other night. Why was he all alone with nobody to turn to? Had he spent his life thinking only about himself and never had time for anyone else? Or was there something else that caused him to become homeless?

How could someone be left all alone in this world with no one to care for them? The thought sent a chill down my spine.

On Saturday morning, I headed to the restaurant that I frequented often. I was meeting a fellow worker there to discuss plans for an upcoming merger. I was hoping I wouldn't get stuck with the teenage waitress who had one bad attitude. She came across tough and made up her appearance to follow suit. I was in no mood to deal with her rude remarks. But as we sat down, this very waitress came sauntering over. My facial expression must have uncovered what I was thinking. After she grudgingly took our order, the woman I was meeting with filled me in on *the rest of the story*. One of her friends was a teacher at the high school and had shared with her the difficulties this young waitress was facing. Her father spent the bulk of his time in a drunken stupor, and her mother walked out on her a few years back. Said she wanted to find a better life for herself. The angry outbursts served their purpose by keeping people at bay and creating a wall she could hide behind. Bullies from school liked to make her their target. She scoffed at their cruel remarks, but their poison arrows touched her heart. She had no one to turn to. She felt rejected and alone. All she wanted was to be loved and to feel like she was important.

Here I was again...wondering why I never took the time to look past her behavior. I should have treated her with kind-

Stephanie Tehan Patterson
Lanark, IL

ness, regardless of how she treated me.

Why hadn't I seen that she was hurting on the inside?

I struggled to fall asleep that night. As I lay there in bed, a movie projector began to play in my mind. Up on the big screen flashed faces of people who had crossed paths with me—people who were hurting. Their outstretched arms were begging for comfort, but I was unaware of their pain. Their sad faces were all too familiar. One was that of an older woman who lived next door—the one I tried to avoid whenever she was out. Her cantankerous attitude pushed people away. But now, her grief and loneliness were being exposed. Her husband used to tell her that when he retired, he would have time to spend with her, and they would travel the world together. But his life was cut short three months prior to retiring...leaving her alone and angry that they were robbed of that time.

The next face I saw was that of a young woman I worked with. She had lost her baby during pregnancy. I remembered passing her in the hall, and she appeared as if everything was fine, so I didn't feel the need to comfort her. I was wrong. Her heart was broken. She and her husband had tried to have a baby for a long time. Finally she got pregnant...only to lose the baby four months later. She was filled with despair. She desperately longed for someone to comfort her and tell her everything was going to be okay.

How could I have thought that everything was okay with her?

The sad, yet familiar faces kept flashing across the screen before me. Suddenly there appeared a multitude of people shuffling about like robots. In their busyness, they would bump into one another...causing them to switch directions. They looked unfocused, as they viewed their world through eyes with tunnel vision. They journeyed alongside one another, but were unaware of the suffering that surrounded them. As I watched this take place, a transparency occurred—exposing all of their secret hiding places. People

Stephanie Tehan Patterson
Lanark, IL

whom I thought were happy and seemed to have it all together were hurting on the inside. Their search for comfort was oftentimes met with rejection.

As the movie projector continued, I saw the face of a young man I met at a recovery center when I was there for a visit. He was in a wheelchair and could no longer walk. He had crashed his motorcycle into a tree and was left paralyzed. The friends he had before the accident drifted away, as they now saw him as a burden who no longer was fun. I remember thinking how amazed I was at his cheerful attitude and his acceptance of his limitations. But it was only a façade. As I caught a glimpse of him up close and personal, I saw that he was filled with despair and had lost his hope for a better life. He had lost his will to go on.

I had this growing desire to reach out and let him know that someone cared.

His face was followed by that of an elderly man in a nursing home whose family had forgotten him. His usefulness to them had ended. The days seemed to last forever, as he hoped that maybe...just maybe...someone would come walking down that hall with outstretched arms...telling him how much they missed him. He waited and waited, but nobody came.

And then there were the faces of children who were suffering silently. Children who were being abused or whose parents had rejected them; children who were starving with no hope for food; children who were being terrorized by bullies...*like my son and the waitress at the restaurant.*

How could this happen? These beautiful children are our future, and it is our job to nurture and protect them.

The projector began to move in slow motion, and I saw a little girl sobbing in the corner. She appeared to be lost. She cried out, but nobody listened. They just walked on by. Her sad cries turned into a whimper. When the projector zoomed in, I saw that the little girl was *me*. And then it was all over.

I was experiencing clashing emotions.

Stephanie Tehan Patterson
Lanark, IL

What was I suppose to understand from all of this?
The following morning brought with it a freshness that I had not felt in a very long time. The vivid scenes from the night before remained, and their purpose was unveiled. Somewhere along my journey, I had parked my dreams and drove off in a different direction...away from where I wanted to be. As a child, I dreamed of doing something important...something that would benefit others. I dreamed of having a happy and close-knit family. But here I was...sacrificing my dreams for the monetary rewards that came with having a prestigious career. I had all the finer things in life...and there was nothing wrong with that in itself...but I did it at a cost. As I continued up the corporate ladder, my job had become my life, and everything else...including my family...had become secondary. I was now this jet setter, rushing from airport to airport, traveling my life away—away from all that was important. My itinerary was packed full, causing me to see my life from my perspective only. I found it difficult to schedule in family time. The friends I hung out with had similar lifestyles. We were all proud of the fact that we could face our demanding schedules with ease and were adept at prioritizing...of course our job was number one. We were able to justify this by making ourselves believe that we were sacrificing for our families, so they could live a life of luxury. The only problem was...they didn't want that. They wanted our time...and that was something we couldn't afford to give them.

Facing this reality was like getting struck by lightning. The jolt of it knocked me out of my complacency. I had lost a lot of years chasing after an ambition that now seemed inconsequential. I was sacrificing for the sake of material possessions and was unmindful of the more valuable blessings I had been given. I kept thinking there would be time enough in the future to enjoy my life, my family, my friends...but the future kept drifting further away. A future that came with no guarantees.

Stephanie Tehan Patterson
Lanark, IL

I had been given an opportunity to see the "big picture" before it was too late. If I had not been granted another tomorrow, would I have been pleased with the path I had chosen? Would I hear my loving God say unto me, "Well done, my good and faithful servant!" or would His face be filled with disappointment? Would I be greeted by people who had gone on before me whose lives were better for having known me? Or would I be standing there all alone?

I had let my life get out of control and now I was faced with having to make a change. It would not be easy, but I had to start...with one step at a time.

I didn't want my legacy to be a mere reflection of material goods that I had once treasured. And the job that I deemed as so important...was only temporal...and it did not define who I was. Yet I had allowed it to do so. It had become the definition of me.

No more!

I felt that old spark of compassion flame up on the inside. It was time to see people in a different light. I had looked at their exterior and judged accordingly, only to miss out on the beauty within. It was time to dig deeper.

My new legacy? It will be that of a loving mother and wife who was there for her friends. When I am thought of, I will be remembered as the person who cared about others—an encourager to the end. I was the one who held the hand of those who were lost and helped them find their way. I rejoiced in their good times and shed tears in their sorrows. I was on the sidelines cheering for every success.

As for my career? Nobody may remember what I did for a living, but they'll surely remember me. I was someone who had made a difference. For once I was lost...but then I was found.

Franklin W. Marshall
Simsbury, CT

Good Earth, Goodbye

Spawn of an obsidian overcast,
shortly after midnight the rain begins,
ticking at the downspout's rim
with the mathematical pulse of a timepiece,
and shortly after midnight begins the sweat
of fear that my maple oak hemlock yew—
may not survive another hour-long downpour of acid;
and under a bridge in Somers the Scantic runs
an ultramarine red—the discolor
of particles shed
from stoves refrigerators automobile parts
rusting upstream in an illicit bankside dump.

Insensate wildlife poachers,
ambush-ready in dastardy for the stampede
that brings into range the game
on an African savannah: locale
for a hecatomb of rhinoceros, an abattoir
for pachyderms, I have yet to experience
that hoofbeat swifter than the wise of a rifle bullet.
Near the equator,
the heat grills the carrion; the vultures
cruise, their crapulence forestalled
by the shouted rodomontade of a would-be
Hemingway: Hey man! Right between the eyes!
What a shot!—
Hemingway, the inglorious: he who made apotheosis of
bovine carnage as sport.
Just once I would like to see the tables
turned; just once I would like to read
how grossly sanguinary the guts of a matador
bleed on the horns of a bull.

Franklin W. Marshall
Simsbury, CT

Ochlocracies of development, of special
interest in fuel lumber minerals livestock;
profit-fisted conspirators in the plot
for ravishment of nature's last preserves;
authors of misfeasance and malfeasance
in the stewardship of bedrock and its genial
mantle, parturient of delphinium
and marsupial, does prevision of the
deletory sequels, if not a reverence for
that life without defense against
your depredations make unnatural demands
upon your conscience? It were better that
a man expire through neglect or violence
than a manatee.

You irruptive hoisters of derricks
on the frangible habitats in Alaska;
you irremissible marauders with engines
that mine green mysteries of Olympia;
you nefarious harvesters of trees that vanish
in the basins of Amazon and Orinoco far
faster than the sunlight of reason
penetrates the timberland of a solipsist;
you multiple scions of a line of baseness
and corruption, where the single parent
is cupidity, in my lifetime I have encountered
few men who are not parasitic on the Earth's
extracted exhumed exhausted treasures,
depositing like troglodytes in their passage
from public lands to private moral sties
the products of insatiable consumption
and blunted intelligence:
metallic offal clinking in the surf
that scours the beaches in Maine;
discarded receipts wrappers brochures that litter the

(continued)

Franklin W. Marshall
Simsbury, CT

camper-trodden valley
of Yosemite; the sludge of a barbecue hurled with
malice aforethought upon a buxom meadow in
Yellowstone.

The end draws near for my archaic
sylvan sanctuaries.

Goodbye Connecticut farmland with your
dew-spangled grasses, the wriggle of your ponds'
amphibians buried under a sleek
beltway of asphalt!
Behind the penultimate piers of a government dam
boom for the final time across the gorge the boisterous
lyrics of white water.

Goodbye, you shadow-secret dells of the Earth,
crying aloud through me for mercy,
but finding none!

***

Sally Belenardo
Branford, CT

Marriage on the Rocks

Many must envy the woman whose spouse
asked her to live with him in a lighthouse.
From a high cliff is the ocean to view,
and she has only light housework to do.

*Goose River Anthology, 2012//*116

Marilyn Zelke-Windau
Sheboygan Falls, WI

Runway

The yellow ginko is having a falling out
with the red maple.
They are both competing
for the year's best runway color.
They've been dressed up, but green,
since spring.
A new designer has altered their look
for the autumn show.
Both sashay with the winsome wind
in October, to please the public judges.
Fickle, yearly, the color of choice
this time is red.
The ginko, feigns interest,
coolly fans her slim limbs,
does a quick shudder,
and exits this year's competition,
promising a return performance.

Elizabeth Tornes
Lac du Flambeau, WI

Why I Write

Two reasons:
first, to see the world lit
by the shimmering blue light
of awareness.

Second, to disappear
so the Creator can see
right through me.

Like a million crickets
singing through my veins,
energy pulses out
until nothing remains

but moonlight
lighting the pages
of the notebook
lying open on the desk.

Jessica Furino
Watchung, NJ

Why Would You Want to Visit Israel!?!

So many people asked me *"Why would I want to visit Israel?"* I was asked if I was afraid. I wasn't, I believed that if God was giving me the opportunity and blessing to go, that I would be safe. We were very safe and felt well protected by the Israeli military. Others asked why I would want to go to a desert? The prophets said that this was a blessed land of milk and honey. The spies that Joshua sent in, brought back grapes that were enormous and pomegranates where the seeds satisfied their thirst for weeks. I believe the *Bible. Israel is the most beautiful country I have ever traveled in and is overflowing with rich landscapes, gentle people, and fragrant, abundant fruits.* I have traveled extensively, and she exceeds anything I have seen in a diversified landscape. Beautiful seas, majestic snow-capped mountains, rugged and colorful desert mountains that compete in beauty and grandeur with the Grand Canyon, deserts and swamps (which no one else wanted transformed into a vast green, fruitful agricultural home.) She has the beautiful, tranquil waters of the Sea of Galilee where Jesus healed thousands in His ministry; a splendid desert that is flanked by the healing Dead Sea. Her history goes back 5,000 years and God has provided her with an arid regional climate (which is blessed with 70 degree weather in February) to preserve all of His holy sites.

I thirsted to touch, smell, see and embrace Jesus' home. I wanted to be in the Holy Land and see the prophets' promises coming true. I wanted to be in the land of milk and honey. Mostly, I sought to walk in our Lord's footsteps and share His ministry. This is what I experienced:

I walked and prayed where the Angel Gabriel asked Mary to birth and raise the Son of God.

I saw the inn where Jesus was born.

I walked in the streets where He played and grew up.

Jessica Furino
Watchung, NJ

I visited and prayed at the wall of the Temple where, at a tender age, He taught the elders about our Father and His home.

I watched and lifted up my brothers and sisters as they renewed their vows in Cana where our Lord performed His first miracle, at the request of His beloved mom.

I basked in the sun as I sat at Tabgha where He fed 5,000 people with five loaves and two fish from a young child's lunch.

I rested and sang praise on a boat, which was a replica of the one He calmed the storm on and gently prodded Peter to walk out on the water to Him, in the Sea of Galilee.

I walked on the banks of the Sea of Galilee and pick up little sea shells and heart-shaped stones while looking at the fat little rock hyraxes, knowing that Jesus may have walked here with His disciples. He may have picked up shells as He shared words of wisdom and His love and compassion for us.

I walked the streets of Capernaum, where Jesus taught and guided His disciples, and I saw Peter's home.

I sat on the hillside, surrounded by gorgeous mustard plants, fragrant, wild rosemary and lavender and imagined I was listening to Jesus speak His Sermon on the Mount, to me.

I prayed in the Temple Mount and listened, in my heart, as Jesus preached my favorite sermon...The Sermon of the Beatitudes.

I realized that Jesus' parables were real stories, as we passed the Inn of the Good Samaritan.

I sat on the rocks and visualized, near the river, Peter, (in Banais, Caesarea) as he makes his confession of faith to Jesus.

I prayed in the Garden of Gethsemane where He rested on the majestic, 3000 year old olive trees.

I walked through Jerusalem through the Via Del Rosa where our Lord carried our burden.

I partook in communion in the Garden Tomb where our

Jessica Furino
Watchung, NJ

Lord rose after three days.

I cringed as I viewed the Valley of Armageddon in Megiddo and imagined the last battle, even though I know He will win.

These are just a few of the things I experienced in this amazing two week pilgrimage.

My question is....*Why haven't you visited this miraculous country?* 50 strangers, who share one faith, left their families and embarked over 10,000 miles to embrace their Lord's home...to see it, to smell it, to feel it, to walk where He walked, to be awed with His presence in this little country. To see and live in His Word or as one of my friends said, "Israel is the *Bible* in 3D." Visiting this blessed country brings history and our Lord's life and ministry...Alive. That is why I visited Israel.

***

Peggy F. Brown
Gray, ME

Simple Gift

You brighten the day with a smile and a wave
Realize what a great gift that you gave?
A smile is contagious and easy to spread
Removing all sadness, worry and dread
Thanks for the gift and have a great day
Spreading cheer in the world is your goal today!

Helene McGlauflin
Bath, ME

December

What is this birth
so many wait for as
darkness and cold
bring us to our knees,
that story of a girl
homeless, blessed
laboring in straw
warmed by beasts
while angels sang
shepherds feared
and kings followed
that star compelling
each to an irresistible
newness?
Even now who can
explain the comfort
of waking after solstice
surrounded, still, by
darkness but changed
by a simple certainty:
light

Judith Thyng
South Portland, ME

Looking Back

Mountains flaunt history by well-worn trails
pine-needle paths where meadows once lay
and cows grazed on a summer day
An abandoned blueberry bush catching the sun
along a stonewall where spiders have spun
Ferns of velvet on nature's walkway
unfolding their leaves in delicate array
Mayflowers spill white on the forest floor
Flooding their splendor briefly once more
Waves rippling across a fresh water lake
long before boats
and motors made wakes
A white steeple lofting above a village green
awakens the spirit of this tranquil scene
A whistle whispers over a rusty track
the ghost of a steam engine calling me back
Indelible images that crowd my thoughts
converge to wrap around my heart

Steve Troyanovich
Florence, NJ

memory ghosts of rio grande
for MW

where are you...now?
it has been so long
since our lips touched
back in that special place
where reality was illusion
and what could not be
could always be...
still your softness
lingers in my dream
while the snow
continues to cover
a faceless earth
and i cannot feel
your warmth
anywhere...

***

autumn sonata

watching the leaves
outside my window
i think of you
bathing in a late
october light
bringing beauty
to a tired place...

Krystal Hatchet
Houston, TX

I Don't Remember His Name

I was headed to Scottsdale for a modeling job and was flying on Southwest where seats are unassigned. Unfortunately, I was in the "C" boarding group and the last passenger to board which means "A" and "B" had already boarded and I would only be left with a middle seat. I never travel with bags that need to go in the overhead compartment, so I only had my purse to shove underneath the seat in front of me. I do not like looking for places to store luggage. I would rather pay the ridiculous fee that the airlines now impose, than to find overhead space above, like a mouse looking for crumbs. I like to sit in the front of the plane as I usually order a vodka cranberry or a cup of chardonnay and want the beverage as soon as I am seated. I like to sit in the front of the plane, because people take too long to retrieve the bags that they squish into bins. On this trip I sat in the 2nd row on the left side of the plane. To my right was a woman in her mid forties, a pretty non-descript white woman with bleached blonde hair and exposed roots that needed to be done, and to my left was an old man. Before I took my seat he moved the newspaper he had been reading that he kept in the middle seat. I am sure that he was hoping that no one would occupy it. As soon as I sat down I looked at his hands, so different from my deep brown smooth pair. Many veins were showing on his hands and arms, forming blue, deep purple roads all across his gentle skin. The color was milky and the skin itself looked very thin and stretched, like a finger nail could pierce it and blood would ooze out. I looked at his nails which were yellow, but well manicured then I looked up and stared at his face. He had shaven, but had small white whiskers jutting out and his lips were dry and a soft deep pink. He had two hearing aids, not the new kind where you can hardly see the device, but the old kind that tried to match a variety of skin tones, but never

Krystal Hatchet
Houston, TX

matched anyone's exact hue. I don't think that he saw me glancing at him and if he did I guess it didn't bother him. I began reading a magazine with the over head light off, because the row behind me had their lights on so I used that glare. The old man admonished me and said, "You should turn on your light, you will strain your eyes." I assured him that I was fine and could see very well using the borrowed light from behind. I then struck up a conversation about why he was travelling. He said that he was going to visit his daughter because he lived in a retirement community in Fort Worth, Texas and his other daughter who lived down the street from him was going to visit friends in New Jersey and he didn't want to be alone. He planned to spend one month in Arizona. I started to wonder about his life so I asked him many questions. He was ninety three years old and lost his wife of over seventy years two years ago. It was during this time that he moved to the retirement facility. He said he took care of his wife in those last years and that he was very depressed when she died. I asked about his daily routine now since he no longer had to care for his dying wife. He said he often woke around 5:30 a.m. and went to bed around 9:00 p.m. He told me that he loved sports and spent a lot of time watching baseball. He said there were many things to do in the facility, but a lot of the residents were very old, in their late nineties so when he did make friends they would often die soon after. Hearing this made me sad, what a lonely feeling that must be. I asked questions about his wife, how they met, and about their life together. They both worked in an automobile factory in the Northeast and were in their early twenties when they met. She had a very feisty personality and was hard working. They had three daughters who all have very different personalities but who all get along. He said he Skyped every Sunday with his girls and this event was the highlight of his week. He was very forthcoming about all of the questions I asked. I asked what it was like growing up during the Great Depression. I always wondered

Krystal Hatchet
Houston, TX

what food was eaten during that time. He said he and his family lived on a farm so they raised pigs and chickens and ate lots of potatoes. Although they never went hungry money was hard to come by and how they didn't have indoor plumbing until he was an adult. Sadly he stated that he was the only one living out of three siblings. When asked if he felt old he said he didn't feel old until his health started failing about one year ago. Even in his eighties he didn't feel old, but he said, "Now I know I am old." I wanted to touch him in a supportive way but chose only to say that I felt that he was "very with it" and that he carried on like he was a man in his sixties. He laughed at that remark. I told him that I had recently turned thirty eight and that my life seems to have gone by so fast. When asked at ninety three did he also feel that way, like life was passing him by he surprisingly said yes. He said his life had gone before his eyes. When asked if he had any regrets he said he didn't think about life like that, he just lived every day and kept living. At this point he signaled that he heard a beep in his ear which meant that the batteries in his hearing aids were running low and he would no longer be able to hear me. I had so much more to talk with him about but he could no longer hear me and the plane was descending.

This man who shared so openly with me about his life and the loss of his true love, made me pause and take notice of my youth, my strength and my future. He helped me to realize that no matter how old you are life is still too short and goes by very quickly. I often think of that April evening and if I had chosen a different seat what the conversation would have been. I made a connection with that man, he touched my heart and I do not remember his name.

Foster B. Meserve, Jr.
Wales, ME

Angels in Our Midst

In this world are special angels
Sometimes we share their road
Although they're like the rest of us
They unknowingly lighten our load

Magically they drift into our lives
Helping guide us along our way
How our paths these angels alter
There's no possible way to say

Although we don't often realize
When our special angels are about
Our lives are thoroughly affected
Leaving us with little doubt

We're all made better people
For having contact with them made
We don't know why they're here
Or the price that they have paid

But when their journey's done
And from this world they pass
It's their fingerprints upon our soul
That make their memories last

Robert B. Moreland
Pleasant Prairie, WI

Cast Irony

Coldest March afternoon, Racine town square,
protest the slaughter, banners tied high to
Civil War memorial, irony.

Oldest son died yesterday, exploded;
raison d'état missing in action!
Union soldier stares east.

It was just a few years ago, youth decried!
High school classmates perished patriotic.
Private, face drawn, weary.

Voices in anger and outrage lifting screams
accusations thick flying, yet now thousands dead!
Statue stands ill at ease.

Rally ends as it began, dispersing beneath
Union soldier, who was someone's son.
Wonder, what was his name?

Moreland, R.B. and Miner, K.M. *Postcards from Baghdad:
Honoring America's Heroes*. Xlibris (Philadelphia, PA, 2008),
page 68.

Idella Anacker
Portage, WI

Just Another Ordinary Day

It was just another day
      the sun rose
      the paperboy was late
      the neighborhood cats cut through
           her backyard on their way home
           from who knows what nighttime adventures
      the neighbors drove by one by one
           on their way to their respective jobs
the kids dragged their feet
           on their way to the bus stop
           backpacks weighing them down
the TV weatherman motioned his way
           through his forecast
           hoping to get it right this time
the squirrels battled the birds
           for food at the feeders
the radio sent out "the greatest music
           ever made"
dogs walked their masters around the block
        routines unbroken, unaltered, unappreciated
           just another ordinary day
              the day she died.

***

On Her Night Table

an empty vase
      a small, child painted, rock
         a line from a poem
"May our house be made of love."

Irene Zimmerman
Milwaukee, WI

Abendlied

When she was a girl, my Austrian mother
spent Sunday afternoons hiking in the mountains
and exploring castle ruins. Visiting her one Sunday
in October, I heard her complain about being
cooped up in a nursing home where outings
were reduced to hallways and nursing stations.

We went for a drive along the Nishnabotna Valley.
As the sun rained lavender and gold over
undulating Iowa hills, she began an *Abendlied*—
an evening song—her voice still clear as the bells
that once sprinkled the Angelus blessing on the corn
and soybean fields surrounding our hometown.

I recalled shelling peas with her on the west porch
one summer evening when I was still a child—
how we both struggled as she determinedly tried
to teach me the song she had learned from her mother
while I vainly attempted to form awkward lips
around strange umlauts and guttural consonants.

As I listened now to the syllables bubbling
from her mouth like a spring in a young river,
I joined my soprano with hers, filling in with la-la-las
where I still stumbled with the *Muttersprache,*
and felt the distance between us dissolve at last
in a wash of lavender and gold.

Sylvia Little-Sweat
Wingate, NC

Final Rites

When songs and words had shaped our grief,
though separate still and desperate on its way
to peace, we crossed a quilt of fields and trees—
like fine, deliberate stitches—to meet the borders
of our own extremities for you had swept beyond
our holding like an autumn seed blown to rest
again on earth—now turned deep and narrow.

Sun and wind were sentinels to your flag-draped
coffin laid by kin for final dedication—no Taps, no
twenty-one-gun salute for one who chose the shadows
of military honor once duty was complete, just a few
simple words a friend scattered like dust on your grave
before the flag was folded for formal presentation.

Only then, though at first unheard, came the birds—
Canada geese in perfect V-formation, missing the one,
flew so low over the tent they interrupted prayer, left
us to stare as they circled then turned toward the sun.

Stephanie J. Batterman
Bath, ME

Mothers

"Why did you let her go? Your own daughter, meetin' boys on street corners. I told you it just ain't proper. A hundred times I said it. Don't you never listen to me, your own mother? I said it ain't decent."

Becca turned from the dishes to face her mother. Let's not go into that again, Ma. Bobbie ain't meetin' a boy on a street corner like you say. Ben is her feller an' she's just meetin' him after work. They're gittin' married soon. Really, Ma, they really are." Becca dropped a glass in the sink. Her hand was shaking.

"Stop doin' those dishes and listen to me. You never did listen to me any. Never could see my side. The Lord knows, I tried. I tried to raise you proper, to be a good mother to you, but you'd never listen to me. You had to have your own way. Never listen to your own mother."

Becca worked furiously in the sudsy water.

"I said listen to me, your own mother. You owe me that at least."

"Oh, Ma, stop it. I don't want to hear it again. Okay, you're a good mother." Becca stopped, remembering all her mother's nagging. "You tried to be a good mother and I'm tryn' to be a good mother to Bobbie. She's a good girl. Let it alone now. Let's just forget it." Becca wrung the dishrag tightly.

"Yeah, just forget it and let her mess up her life the way you messed up yours. Lord knows, I tried to raise you proper. But, no, you had to have a mind of your own. You wouldn't listen to me. Oh, no! You had to get into a mess. You wouldn't even marry Harry when he asked you.

"He was a good man, better than you deserved. He would 'a married you even though you was in a mess. But, oh, no, you wouldn't even save your own decency. And what of me? Look at the shame you caused me. No, never a thought for

Stephanie J. Batterman
Bath, ME

for me, your own mother. Why didn't you marry Harry?"

"I told you, Ma, I didn't love Harry. I loved Bob."

"Love! Ha! What good did love do you?"

"Ma, I did love him."

"A dead man?"

"Don't, Ma. I did love him. I never believed that he was dead. Not in my heart. I always hoped they made a mistake. I always hoped he would come home. I promised him I'd wait."

"They told you he was dead. Even had a funeral for him. How could you go on loving a dead man? 'Specially when he got you in a mess. You can bet he didn't love you. If he did he'd 'a loved you like a decent man, like Harry. You could 'a married him. But, no! You had 'a love a dead man who couldn't marry you no more. You could 'a saved your name and given Bobbie one. You couldn't even think of your own mother and her shame. No, you had to love a dead man!"

"Shut up, Ma! Just shut up! Becca's insides were shaking and she winced as her teeth bit into her lip. Tears burned her eyes. She felt the wet suds trickle between her fingers and down her wrist. The dishrag crushed in her fist made her fingernails white and her fingers felt numb.

She carried the dishpan to the back porch and dumped the dirty water over the railing. The water splashed a lone pink flower that looked lost in the otherwise brown yard. She looked down the row of identical black porches which resembled ragged afterthoughts to the tumble-down houses.

She wished she hadn't yelled at her mother, but the argument was too familiar. She was just so tired, so tired of hearing the same thing day after day. She'd like just one word, just one good word from her mother. How she hated living here; hated that row of dark houses. Sometimes she wanted to leave, just run away from it all.

She leaned over the railing and gazed at the lone flower blooming there. It was always getting hit with dirty dishwater, but still it grew in that ugly place.

Stephanie J. Batterman
Bath, ME

She sat on the broken step. If she had married Harry, at least she could have left this place. But she never could leave Bob, even though she knew that he was really dead. She remembered with a twinge how she had hated him for a moment when she learned that he was dead, leaving her with her secret inside. She had hated him again when the baby was born. But she had never been able to forget him, never been able to let go of the love they had had. All she had were the memories and her child, Bobbie. But it was the memories that sustained her; the memories of his kisses and the way he held her and playfully mussed with her hair.

That had always reminded her of when she was a little girl and had sat on her daddy's knee. He had always played his fingers on her cheek like a piano and she had laughed. But her mother had always been mad when she sat on Daddy's lap. She tried not to laugh when he played his fingers on her cheek so her mother wouldn't get mad. But she always did. Then her mother would yell at her and make her go outside and play in the dirt. She'd listen to her mother yell at Daddy and tell him not to touch her.

He said, "She's our girl, my little girl...what's wrong with you?"

Then her mother would yell some more about not touching her. Pretty soon, Daddy left.

Her mother never touched her. She remembered how wild her mother had been when she brought Bob home, and he had held her hand. Her mother had flown into a rage and sent him away.

After that she had met Bob late at night, after her mother was asleep. He made her feel little again and warm and safe, like when Daddy had been there. But he had died and now she had Bobbie...and her mother.

The houses were disappearing into the shadows of the evening and the bony porches were silhouetted against the reddish sky.

Becca got up and went back into the house. Her mother

Stephanie J. Batterman
Bath, ME

was slouched into her rocking chair in a dark corner of the kitchen. Becca walked over to her and looked at the pale wrinkled face that must have been pretty once.

She wondered what it would be like to touch her mother. She reached out her hand, but it was shaking. Suddenly she realized that she wanted to hit her, wanted to hate her.

She ran out the back door and down the broken back steps. In front of her was the little pink flower, alone in the dirt. She picked it tenderly and stood in the gathering darkness with the flower pressed tightly to her cheek where it was bathed with her tears.

***

Steve Troyanovich
Florence, NJ

shadow and lullaby

> *Dont le corps de toujours est braise*
> *Et le coeur, racine d'aube*
> —Serge Sautreau

through the fingers of silence
you enter my heart
shadow and lullaby
at the edge of stillness…
i dream wrapped
inside the universe
of your eyes—
holding the moonlight
touching your face

Elmae Passineau
Wausau, WI

Seven Grooms for Lil

Well, number seven was eighty-eight when he bit the dust,
Thrown from his horse, a temperamental roan name
      o' Gus.

Number six, the short one, caught his heel in a sidewalk
       grate,
Cracked his head soundly and the ambulance arrived too
       late.

Lucky number five passed on peacefully in a soft bed
But not, scandalously, next to the woman he had wed.

Number four ingested poison, it was over quickly,
Years later, people still speculated suspiciously.

The handsome one, number three, charmed every woman
       in town,
Shocked them all when from the rafters they took his body
       down.

Lost soul number two with hobo wanderlust in his veins,
The dread report finally came, a fatal leap, two trains...

The first one, they were only seventeen at the altar,
Love pledged eternal lasted eleven months, no better.

The lady's eighty now with a beau of forty named Will,
If you're the betting kind, I'd put my money sure, on Lil.

Maryann Hurtt
Elkhart Lake, WI

What Dementia Did Not Steal

for years
my uncle greeted me
with his kiss on each cheek
French embrace
I learned how to tilt my head
so our choreographed love
danced just right
he's old now
sometimes here, sometimes there
he stares across the room
when I walk in
not quite sure who this person is
he rises from his chair
ataxic legs
wobble under him
our heads sway true
and for a little bit
everything is good again

Sally Woolf-Wade
New Harbor, ME

Empty Swings

Eye sockets
of the house
are lifeless.
No candles shine out
on the December lawn
that once blazed
with lighted
reindeer displays
in the Christmas season.

Two swings
hang limp
from the twisted oak
one a wooden plank
the other an old tire
next to the sign:
Foreclosure—
Auction tomorrow
ten a.m.

Rozell Caldwell
Brownsville, TN

Homeless

Each night as I write by candlelight
I hear the sound of a ghost
Knocking gently on my neighbor's door

It's after midnight
The cold key turns gently
He enters noiselessly

Silence returns
The landlady is watchful
But she cannot see

The boarder who leaves before noon
But is back much too soon
Knocking softly

***

Daniel Jamieson
Candler, NC

Mona Lisa

Mona Lisa, Mona Lisa
They have named you
Even though I know
Your name is
Esther Schwartz

Anne L. Hess
Stillwater, ME

Velvet Hunter

There was no time for stealth, and the little stalker leaped down from her perch not with soft gliding paws but with the thump of four potatoes hitting a drum.

Only with human eyes adapted to the dark night could she be seen, and then only as a darker version of blackness. Her own eyes, of course, saw her realm clearly, and her over-long whiskers let her sense it just as keenly. Her fur flowed gracefully through the air like feathers settling from a rup-tured pillow as she launched into flight. With her fully dilat-ed black pupils, she maneuvered deftly around the obstacles placed carelessly by the humans with whom she lived, deign-ing to tolerate the clutter that scarcely resembled the jungle that existed in her imagination. She glided around a door (cave), a hassock (palmetto cluster), a chair leg (bamboo stalk) and tricycle (tree stump), under a table (fallen tree branch) and behind the cooking island (mass of vines), past the dish of kibble (dried carrion) and past the shoe tray (river pebbles). She slid through the cat-size window gap as if it were as wide as goal posts, the sides raking tiny wisps of loose fur as her torso skimmed gracefully through with only the faintest swish of the flap.

This time she dropped down to the porch floor with the grace of Baryshnikov, silent and menacing as she tracked the sounds of a creature (maybe a baby zebra or wildebeest) invading her territory. Her whiskers were full out, her ear tufts soared like ship masts and her feet moved like marsh-mallows across the hard wood floor, undaunted by the minuscule bits of sand and ash tracked in by the human boots in winter. No great cat lets small things get in the way.

The emboldened rodent never had a chance, believing erroneously that its stash of bird seed was an unguarded supermarket in a gated neighborhood. It scuttled along with abandon, chittering innocently as it made for the mouse-buf-

Anne L. Hess
Stillwater, ME

fet in the corner of the milk porch, the plastic bucket long since penetrated with two tiny holes that leaked the tasty morsels. It paused reflexively to sniff, its whiskers twitching busily but revealing no hazards. Creeping along the corner of the paint-flaked wall, over the rain-warped linoleum towards the tantalizing bouquet of sunflower hearts, finch seeds and nut bits that no self-respecting rodent could resist, the trusting creature slowly approached the food and, unknowingly, its fate.

The twin radar-dome ears tracked the prey silently in a motionless body akin to a stone statue, poised with every muscle as tense as a loaded gun ready to fire in a millisecond. Then a slight movement, one foot forward and then another, the sinuously-waving tail hovering in a delicate balancing act with the feet, a furry statue poised between each step. Another foot, placed daintily so as not to squeak the floorboards, nostrils wide and ears forward to listen intently to the breathing and chewing sounds of the mouse, sounds beyond the ken of paltry human ears. Closer, closer.

The attack was a brutal blur, the outcome predetermined and grisly. The hunter pounced adroitly onto the hapless nibbler, grinding the scimitar blades attached to its feet into the tender fur and paper-thin skin of the unsuspecting mouse. The creature barely had time to emit the softest of peeps before its windpipe was shut down and it began that last struggle for its life.

As if in a moment of contrition, the hunter released its grip. The mouse, stunned first by the attack and then by its freedom, hunkered down in shock, not appreciating that this was a short window of opportunity. It gathered its wits and ran towards its escape hole, but Hunter intercepted it with a disarmed paw, pushed the wounded mouse towards the porch and watched it run for a fateful ten seconds. She made a second approach, this time to watch with morbid fascination as the creature fled in panic and circled frantically to find its way out. There was none, of course, but the mouse

Anne L. Hess
Stillwater, ME

brain is too small to reason at all, much less as quickly as needed to devise and execute Plan B.

There might have been thirty seconds left in the life of the victim—extended a few seconds by the grace of the hunter or the tenacity of its spirit—and whether to succumb to heart failure or the killing blow did not matter in the end. The brevity of life might have passed through its little brain, or not, but its only response of flight and survival had been long ago incorporated into its genetic blueprint.

To the hunter, those thirty seconds passed slowly, requiring more patience than expected even for her own kind. She had to make sure the creature was healthy enough to eat and only recently deceased, thus ensuring a luscious meal or worthy tribute. Meals are tastier than tributes, of course, but sometimes even a human would respect what the little hunter could contribute to the pride. Everyone should do their share, her ancient DNA told her.

Depending on your point of view, the demise of the mouse was either beautiful and swift, or gross and repulsive. Hunter grasped the mouse's windpipe firmly and held it until all movement stopped, as is the way of her kind; only then did she decide what to do with it.

Eat, she decided: Fresh meat is hard to come by. She chewed in a silence broken by the soft crunch of bones and tearing of skin and sinew, sounds audible only to the finely-tuned ear. The humans were in other rooms sleeping in their protected cocoons, oblivious to the surreptitious violence within their household, not that they could have seen or heard the events even if they'd been awake.

Hunter enjoyed her gruesome meal, savoring the juicy, bloody bites, until almost every shred of the victim had been eradicated. She blithely licked up each spatter of blood and tissue from the porch floor, every bit of fur and flesh. She left only a small tribute, a poker-chip-sized tuft of blooded, fleshy fur which she carried carefully and laid beside the dining table, trusting it would be found at the next human's meal.

Anne L. Hess
Stillwater, ME

Then she lay under the table (thick forest canopy) and began cleaning herself, as systematically and thoroughly as an obsessive housewife who is determined to eliminate every living thing within a half-mile. Hunter licked each strand of her silky fur, removing all traces of gore with the rough sandpaper of her tongue, rinsing with the moisture of her saliva, and chewing delicately with her teeth as she sucked tiny drops into her mouth. She twisted herself like a Chinese contortionist to reach all the parts of her body regardless of whether there might be a scrap of soil on them, and proceeded from fore-paws to abdomen to hind-paws, down her back to the tip of her wispy tail, and gnawed the cuticles of every claw. After thirty minutes she was immaculate to the highest feline standard; not good enough for fastidious humans, of course, who had the expectation that their pets should be just as sterile as themselves.

Now fully morphed back into her pet persona, the gentle Hunter padded softly through the house, up the stairs and into the softly-lit room, snuggled down with her youngest human on the cozy little bed with its pink and purple flowers, content to sleep in watchful peace. Her soft purrs comforted the unsuspecting child and coaxed a few more blissful hours of dreaming. The girl dreamed of lollipops and bouncing balls, Hunter of African savannah and antelopes.

"Ewww, what's that?" the five-year old human cried when she spotted Hunter's ghastly tribute lying on the floor at breakfast-time. The girl immediately started to pick it up, fascinated more than repulsed by the scrap.

Mother dashed to the spot, then bent over to examine, from a hygienic distance, the small bit of gray fur edged in dark red. She determined that it had once been alive, was dangerous, and promptly seized it daintily in the tips of two fingers protected by a paper napkin. She hastily wrapped it in a paper towel and put it in the trash with a scornful "Ugh!"

Anne L. Hess
Stillwater, ME

"I don't know about that cat of ours," she said to her husband when he came down the stairs. "She brings the most awful things, I don't know where she finds them!"

"Well, it was probably a mouse or something she found outside."

"But she doesn't go outside any more, remember?"

"Right. Must have been from inside, then. Maybe it's good she's trapping those things, keeping our house clear of mice and stuff," Dad said.

"Maybe, but I don't like thinking about *that*," Mother replied.

Watching warily from the doorway, Hunter saw that her tribute was not appreciated, and she rued her failings as a teacher of humans. She knew she had no failings as a hunter; perhaps someday her humans would understand, she mused in her cat's wise way as she sauntered back to her sentry's perch where she would entertain visions of wildebeest and rabbits until Baby Girl came looking for play.

***

P. C. Moorehead
North Lake, WI

Seeding

How does a seed
become a tree?
I love you.

George Wentz
Sturgeon Bay, WI

Feeding the Pigeons

A small boy, I stopped to watch
the old man sitting on a bench
feeding the pigeons
at the Lincoln Park Zoo.

His nose no longer to the grindstone
nor his shoulder to the wheel,
he sat alone, his days empty.
Still he found a reason for being—

The plump grey birds
were grandmotherly
as they arrived in a flutter
and cautiously strutted around.

They waited for the old guy
to reach in his paper bag,
bring out a couple of peanuts
and toss them on the ground.

The world of importance
spun around them
and no one cared about
the old man and his pigeons.

Yesterday at the Lincoln Park Zoo
the pigeons were waiting, and
there was a small boy watching
as I tossed peanuts from my paper bag.

Maryann Hurtt
Elkhart Lake, WI

Glass Bottles and Ice

On a just right day
they went to the canal
an endless ice ribbon
stretched next to the Potomac
and skated for miles

hands behind his back
her father swayed rhythmic strides
and told young boy stories
how he delivered milk
glass bottles in canvas bags
blades strapped to shoes
on ice covered Iowa streets

fifty years later
she sees his old man stooped ways
wonders how he remembers
the balance
of glass bottles and ice
and if memory
of flight while still grounded
to earth
is enough

Patrick T. Randolph
Murphysboro, IL

Songs Touching Ears

A snowflake's gentle laughter on my wife's jacket sleeve
Makes her ears grow into attentive giggles, and she calls
To me and I come running to listen to other snowflakes
        falling,
Making the same soft whispered laughter, a chorus of
        sky-songs.

We stand now under night's white world, our grinning teeth
Holding out their arms to embrace these small snowflakes
And their talent for causing our souls to come together and
        our
Hands to hold each other and swing like children
        discovering
That the universe of elation is always a moment like this—
                                        of birth grinning infinity.

***

A Winter Path on the Farm

Horse tracks in the snow—
Frigid morning air—crisp breeze—
Rooster's crow starts time;

Sun appears above the barn—
The horse still walks in warm dreams.

Goose River Anthology, 2012//148

Toni Ortner
Brattleboro, VT

The Story of Your Life

The story of your life
Is not who you are.
You are much larger than your story.

Stop telling yourself the same words today
you said yesterday.

You believe your story is you.

You say you can't stop the bleeding
when there are sponges all around.

You are not the story you tell yourself.
The story of your life is an old moldy hat.
Throw it out.

Admit you do not know the plot.

***

I Think of Eichmann

I think of Eichmann
thin mild-mannered
sitting in his cell surrounded by armed guards
convinced he did his duty to his Fuhrer.

The door clangs shut
The gas fills the showers.
They meet Death, soap in hand.

J. Adams
Edgecomb, ME

Pemaquid Point Evening

The sun sets low
The moon comes up
Waves crash hard
Against the rocks below.
The light flashes high
The sailor to warn
Stay far away or your
Ship will be torn
The moon beams cast
A cold, lonely glow
On sailors and ships
And ocean below
The island sets stately
On the horizon so still
Awaiting a fog horn or
Ship's whistle shrill
Lighthouses afar blinking
Their patterns to guide
Ships like stars in
The inky, black sky
The ocean is angry and
Roars in the night
Waves crash the rock
'Neath the cold moon's light.

Carol Kramer
New York, NY

Bedelia

Bedelia was 10 years old when she arrived in the summer of 1966. She was a gift to my older sister Betty and me from my dad, Adam, the auto mechanic. She wasn't beautiful, but she was ours. Turquoise and white with a manual transmission, she was our own Chevy BelAir sedan. She had that old car smell, like a utility closet that had been ignored for a decade mixed with fuel oil that wasn't fully combusted. Clearly there were no emission standards in 1966. Bedelia was an accomplice to many unshared stories, but I knew, given her age, she must have been to many drive-in movies and worn lots of popcorn kernels and miscellaneous wrappers in the folds of her seats. She was, and would always be, discreet.

Neither Betty nor I had a driver's license. She failed her road test only because she couldn't parallel park, make a three-point u-turn and stay in her own lane. I had just received my learner's permit and was anxious to hit the road. Adam was determined to stop playing chauffeur to his teenage daughters. Mom never did get her license, being thwarted by learning from Adam and suffering from "recurrent depression" most of her life. She would gladly have driven us anywhere, rather than let us roam around eastern Long Island unsupervised. Adam didn't have the same concerns. Stacey, my best friend since second grade, had already passed her road test, so she was to be the designated licensee in the car while the two novices took time at the wheel. Adam, a member of the Riverhead Police auxiliary, ignored the fact that Stacey only had a junior license so this wasn't legal. We all gladly ignored it too.

Stacey was orphaned at seven as revealed by her own words: "My mom checked out by gas fumes in my uncle's garage." She lived with different family members throughout her childhood, but this summer, she lived with us. It was

Carol Kramer
New York, NY

perfect. It meant that she wouldn't have to climb out of her window at her uncle's house and jump off the roof to go to the bars on Dune Road in Westhampton, Long Island with us. Bedelia, always ready for adventure, would get us to our destination illegally as we used photocopied phony IDs to enter the bars. The drinking age was 18 then, but if you looked 16, any ID was a ticket to party.

Dune Road in the 1960's was a narrow unlit way leading to a handful of very popular hangouts full of party goers, mostly older and more experienced than the three Mercy High School teens in Bedelia. Bars aside, the road often flooded as the bay or the ocean rose to cover portions of it. On top of that, notorious fog often engulfed the road. It was such a night that Betty became our pilot at the wheel. She was struggling to see the road ahead with her corrected 20-800 vision while faithful Bedelia followed her rambling directions. The dune grass and reeds were all around us. Suddenly the sound of splashing water mixed with sand over the hood, followed by a complete halt, was anything but comforting. The silence of the engine finally stopped Stacey, Betty and I from laughing long enough to acknowledge that we might be in trouble. There was nothing we could do but wait. There were no cellphones, we had no triple A, and we were driving illegally, but we knew we'd get out of this somehow. No intellectual discussions were taking place inside Bedelia. The time was well-spent trying to come up with possible excuses for why we were in this predicament. How could we BS our way out of it and avoid trouble, should the need arise. We made every attempt to stay clear of the macabre. "Who might be roaming through the tall dune grass on a dark, deserted, foggy flooded road?" were thoughts that were unspoken that night. To our good fortune, no police patrol or pervert happened along during our scheming. After what seemed hours, Bedelia finally took a deep breath, sputtered and fired up her V-8 engine. We backed away from the dune. No time left for the bars, we humbly limped back to

Carol Kramer
New York, NY

Riverhead with Stacey at the wheel. Nobody was waiting up for us, so we quietly went upstairs to bed.

In the morning Adam decided that it was time to give the engine a check. He was always concerned that Bedelia was safe for the girls in their illegal travels. The inevitable question arose: "Why is there sand on the battery, the radiator, and in every conceivable place under the hood?" Betty and I went blank as Stacey with her quick wit filled the silence: "We went through a puddle, a ver-r-r-y big puddle." All those hours of deliberation had yielded a simple acceptable answer for my dad.   The fact that the question was answered by Stacey made it more plausible. To this day, Stacey claims that "I was your father's favorite." I agree, and I still thank her for that. I also know that he was her favorite fill-in father, the one that lived long enough to laugh and look the other way at certain indiscretions.

As for Bedelia, she remained the secret, silent accomplice, who miraculously kept us unharmed during our crazy teenage years.

***

Patrick T. Randolph
Murphysboro, IL

Happy Cow

A young cow moves closer to the farm house,
Is it the silhouette of the farmer
Hugging his wife in the morning kitchen
That makes this cow sway her tail with a smile?

Sylvia Little-Sweat
Wingate, NC

Truce

"You really show how much you
love me," the mother hurled like
a poisoned dart at her daughter's
heart. Then like rags they rent
the love just spoken—each more
broken by relinquished care.

Since birth their boundaries had
been drawn by a mother—herself
motherless since a child—who
demanded full worth of measured
love and made "If I had a mother"
her battle cry against the hurt.

They hugged their resentments
like winter coats against the chill
of dying day, still enraged by love's
equation—Don't go = I can't stay.
Both knew those words in time would
rearrange in the cruel math of death.

Belva Ann Prycel
Alna, ME

The Great Horseshoe Tournament

Leaning against the wall of our garage in Maine is a rusted set of horseshoes, ones that have moved with my husband and me to the many homes and coastal settings we have lived over the years. Dusty and paint-chipped they sit amid the lawn equipment, tools, used furniture, and assorted paraphernalia of our lives. Yet each time I pass them I see a gravelly playing court and that miraculous summer when I learned that improbable possibilities were more accessible than I ever believed, where the implausible could actually be within my reach.

This wisdom was most surely learned through the auspices of my Uncle Bob, a playful soul—a six foot three, orange-haired, wiry jester of a man with a talent for spontaneity and feckless humor. Happily, the ocean-swept summers of my childhood were marvelously gifted by his unique presence, for Bob and his wife, Mary Emma, owned a small beach house just a few blocks from my parents' cottage. There I would aimlessly wander on restless days, determined to divert Bob from his many tasks. And I knew Bob could always be counted on to relish the moment and drop any chore to surf the waves or play a game of horseshoes.

You could say that in the latter he was considered something of an expert, at least by the men in the neighborhood, and his throw was unerring and bizarre, a work of art in motion, for he held the shoe with the tips of his fingers ever so lightly on one prong, and somehow when released the shoe would mysteriously make a halfturn in midair, floating arrestingly toward the stake. For years I tried to duplicate his throw and could never do it. And each time I lost another game, I would endure his effusive teasing. Still, I haplessly persisted.

I think it was about the time I turned thirteen that the next door neighbor, Mr. Johnson, jokingly suggested (after

Belva Ann Prycel
Alna, ME

losing multiple games of horseshoes himself to Bob) that he would offer a monetary reward if anyone could beat the red-haired wonder. I don't remember what figure he offered. It was likely insignificant. But my own ego was piqued enough that I took up the challenge.

So it was that summer, in the pursuit of what seemed patently impossible, that I doggedly advanced. My father noticed my strange persistence at the horseshoe court, seeing me working at my swing every night after dinner, and he eventually assumed the role of ally and instructor. He had probably come closer than anyone else to besting Bob on several occasions, and thus our little effort began, humbly at first, but intensifying as the summer progressed.

I should relate that my father's horseshoe pitch was not at all like Bob's, for he held the shoe firmly in the curve of the "U" and threw it straight, end over end, till it flipped and slid neatly into, or near, the pole. As for me, I could master neither my father's nor Bob's technique, and eventually settled into my own—a single, controllable rotation that could make a slide or catch the stake in midair, sometimes spinning and hooking the bar, or sometimes unfortunately slipping off if it connected too high. What was needed, I eventually intuited in my childish brain, was some perfect form of muscle memory—something like the kind needed when playing the piano—the right amount of pressure in the flick of the wrist, the right dead-eye aim, the focused concentration coupled with an exact angle of lift and loft. In my chase for precision I labored, every day, practicing with my father as my mother did dishes and watched from the kitchen window.

That summer we set up our horseshoe court on the edge of the gravel driveway, between our house and Mr. Johnson's property. The Johnsons had a second floor apartment with a long outside stair leading up to a small landing and this proved a perfect viewing platform. Mr. Johnson, an elderly man who smoked Chesterfields and had once been a champion swimmer, sat on the top steps and daily observed our

Belva Ann Prycel
Alna, ME

progress. My father and I always practiced till the sun sank below the distant marshes and the first mosquitoes appeared at dusk and drove us back inside.

But it was more than mosquito bites I noticed, for as the weeks progressed, my hands were changing. They had become as calloused as a lumberjack's, and my right arm had developed a bizarre lump I later learned was something called "a bicep." Regarding the rest of me, there were bruises and scratches on my thigh where the horseshoes scraped my leg, and my right shoulder hurt every time I threw. I don't know how to describe my emotional condition, my state of mind, except to say I was probably engaged in the closest thing to a compulsion that I would ever experience in childhood. I was an unathletic pubescent girl, but I was determined to beat Bob at a game in which I had suffered his relentless teasing for years. I also knew I wanted to be good at one sport to earn the approval of my father—and he and I were surely bonded that summer in a mutual quest. I was going to do my best to win it.

Throughout July I worked on my swing, on lining up the stake between the prongs of the shoe, then holding the target in this sightline when it left my outstretched hand. I became something like a surveyor then, or an aeronautical engineer, calculating distance and thrust and energy required to reach the iron stake thirty feet away. To the probable consternation of neighbors, the peace of the beach was disrupted by the noisy ping-cla-clang-ping of the horseshoes, the clash of metal on metal, and all the grating and banging overwhelming the crash of waves on the nearby shore.

Sometimes Bob would stop by to observe, or my father, Bob, myself, and Mr. Johnson would play a team game. Bob and my father always earned the highest score—that was, until August. By then I could hold my own with the men.

A milestone was reached then when my father told me he wasn't going to practice with me anymore; I should "just keep at it" and work on my own. I confess I was getting confident

Belva Ann Prycel
Alna, ME

and pretty good then, stacking up horseshoes like dancers round a maypole, sliding them into the stake or nailing high-flying ringers in one out of three throws. But then one day Uncle Bob stopped by and threw a ringer of his own....

I saw him standing beside the driveway, quizzically looking at the court, pacing out the distance between the stakes. When my father and I questioned this activity, he announced, rather gravely, that the court was "only set at a paltry thirty feet—and not the official regulation of forty."

Good grief, I thought! That was nearly the entire length of our driveway! My whole muscle memory technique was predicated on that distance. The victory began disappearing before my eyes.

Then, as such things fortuitously happen, Mr. Johnson, who had been watching this scenario from his perch above, came to the rescue.

Scratching his few thinning shreds of hair, choosing his words carefully, he observed that for "public safety" (those passing on the street who could dangerously connect with an overshot horseshoe) a "more prudent" thirty feet was surely desirable. Plus, he reasoned, we had "used that distance all summer without complaint," and it was "only fair to maintain it."

Ahah. Mr. Johnson's logic was both reasonable and impeccable. And besides, I knew he was a used car salesman and good at persuasion.

Uncle Bob relented, and the game was set for Sunday, Labor Day Weekend.

I couldn't eat anything that day. I didn't even go to the beach for a swim. I was too enervated and I spent the entire morning practicing.

My father carefully prepared the court, testing the stakes and pounding them securely into the ground, then packing and leveling a small circumference around each pole.

Late in the afternoon Mr. Johnson and his houseguests

Belva Ann Prycel
Alna, ME

positioned themselves, along with their coolers of beer, on the stairs beside the court. Our neighbors, the Gigliardis, the Smiths, the Webbers, all carried beach chairs from across the street and got comfortable. My friend Joanne and her cousin Billy and his little brother Donny arrived, blowing bubble gum, and dragging their inner tubes and canvas rafts as seat cushions. My parents were there, as well as a small crowd of summer renters. Bob drew a "throwing" line in the sand where we could stand behind the stakes and we nervously took up our positions, side by side.

"Well, you ready to get beat?" Bob teased, snorting and laughing as he always did.

I looked steadily back at him. "No Uncle Bob...are *you* ready to get beat?"

"Ha, hah!" came the retort, "You want a couple of practice shots?"

Maybe he was giving me some kind of advantage, but I took it. "Sure" I said, but not wanting to appear too eager, "you go first."

"Okay," he agreed. Then, as I watched incredulously—he immediately and devastatingly threw a ringer.

I considered this opening salvo utterly abysmally, then quakingly and hesitantly stepped up and threw my first shoe.

It looked all right at first...straight in line...but it embarrassingly overshot the top of the stake by a foot and went rolling end over end toward the street. Little Donny Teefee, a devilish eight-year-old, quickly jumped up and gleefully chased it.

I surveyed the amused faces around me, steadied my trembling arm, and tried to tell myself to focus.

"Hah! You had too many Wheaties this morning, Belva Ann!" ribbed Bob, doubling over with laughter as Donny retrieved the shoe.

"Yea....I guess so...." I said, already despondent and wondering if I was up to this venture.

Belva Ann Prycel
Alna, ME

Well, inevitably the first game was a definitive loss. It belonged to Bob. I was simply too nervous, trying too hard, and it took me the whole game to start to relax and begin to find my old muscle memory. I made a few ringers, even topped one of Bob's, giving me the sum of both, but he still won the overall game handily.

Then came game two.

I tried to concentrate, gradually remembering my form then, feeling a small resoluteness growing inside me. I knew I could do this, knew I wanted to honor my father after all the effort he had put into this. And I didn't want to embarrass myself or my friends.

I tried to pretend there was no one there, that it was just Bob and me, that the only reality was the moment, the horseshoe court, the game. I recall the whole thing began to feel hypnotic, as though the only thing that existed was the stake, the feel of the shoe as it left my hand, and the suspended breathing as metal scribed the air—then the cla-clang of a solid hit followed by the sound of applause. It was all trancelike, mesmerizing, and I'd never felt such control before.

I remember we were both hitting ringers then in two out of four throws. Mr. Johnson and my father were yelling and cheering. The beers flowed, and the soda popped. People laughed and clapped, egging us on.

Bob was serious suddenly, and I was glad. I wanted to win this thing squarely, honestly, or not at all. I knew he certainly wasn't cutting me any slack, and I didn't want any. In my mind we were equals now, at least in this endeavor, and I felt an unimaginable pride. Then, almost like a miracle, I topped Bob's last ringer and won game two....

What a shock! Unexpected! Everyone grew suddenly quiet. The atmosphere had thickened, shifted.

We both hunkered down...there was only one final game to go.

My father stepped in and straightened the battered

Belva Ann Prycel
Alna, ME

stakes, then took a broom and a trowel and leveled the rutted court. Bob rubbed dirt on his hands and spit on the horseshoes for luck. I shook the blood down into my hands as Mr. Johnson's half-blind collie dog wandered across the gravel and Joanne grabbed him and held his collar.

Bob suddenly turned to me, "You're doin' real good there, Belva Ann."

"You too, Uncle Bob," I gratefully offered back.

Then we began again.

We cla-clanged through game three. Bob threw, and I followed. We both layered shoes close to, or onto the stake. Equal for equal.

Then, at the last round, Bob hefted a shoe that missed the stake by a mere quarter inch. My chance!

Mr. Johnson stooped down to measure the distance and declared it was not quite "on."

But immediately I threw a shoe that bounced on Bob's and knocked it onto the stake, (with mine atop.) Suffice it to say that Bob had one ringer, and I had claimed it! The game just might be mine.

Bob studied the situation for a long time. This was critical.

He slowly went up to the line and I thought he looked impossibly poised and assured in his sinewy, long-limbed confidence. Then, by some unknown wizardry, he flung that amazing twisting shoe of his into the air. I can still see it lifting and arching and turning in weightless suspension…then coming down and neatly slamming the pole. Bob had just, in the most devastating way, piled a wringer on top of mine. He had claimed all three wringers.

It was surely a sobering thing, and I was vaguely aware that people were cheering. But some were quiet, especially my beach friends. They probably thought I was toast. I confess that for me, a sense of futility co-existed oddly with a remote sense of possibility that seemed to hang over the court.

Belva Ann Prycel
Alna, ME

Nobody made a sound as I stepped up to the line and squinted through the black prongs of my shoe. In the U-shaped scope I could see them: three ringers...with just an inch of metal pole peering atop it all. So much was at stake.

I suppose that I decided then, or rather felt in some wordlessly instinctive way, that there was no room for equivocation in this throw, no halfway to this effort. Everything had come down to this. It had to be high, it had to hit squarely, and if I missed, the shoe would flip off into oblivion. I would lose the game.

It was a strange sensation to be standing there, feeling eerily vulnerable yet centered, like I could command the shoe by my will, follow it with my mind's eye—compel it to fly through the air, will it to the stake, will it to land. So I did what I had done all summer—I concentrated, lined the post up three times between the prongs, and threw. I tried to give just a fraction more lift as I cast.

It seemed that time virtually stopped. The shoe exited my hand and rolled over in a kind of slow motion spin. I watched it scribe a perfect arc, a single beautiful turn, the prongs headed straight for the stake. It was in my control, right in line, riding high, holding steady, floating down, and then...CLA-CLANG! It connected with the top of the pole like it had been anchored with an invisible hand, sticking the landing like a gymnast!

Around me there was stunned silence, disbelief, then I began to hear shouts and cheers rising from the small crowd. Mr. Johnson slapped me hard on the back. Bob gave me my first handshake, then a hug. My father beamed. Our aging neighbor, Smitty, was shaking his balding head, "Never saw no girl do that before." What an amazing day—and it went into our family history for years as the "Great Horseshoe Tournament."

I really don't remember what we all did afterwards. I probably went off to play with my friends and relish the joy of victory. But I do know that in the summers after, we all

Belva Ann Prycel
Alna, ME

played again, and often. Sometimes I beat Uncle Bob, some-times not. Happily through the years my father and Uncle Bob recounted the story at family gatherings, and I viewed it as one of the singular achievements of my young life.

So I guess it's not surprising that I saved the old horse-shoes and have traveled with them over the years. It is good to have these touchstones of memory. Sometimes when I pass them in the garage, I like to pick one up, get the feel of the metal between my thumb and forefinger, and give a little toss toward some imaginary stake. It all comes back again. And when I do I see a gravelly playing court and hear the cheers rising and fading in the distance—and I remember once again the unbounded joy of implausible possibilities.

***

Robert Erickson
Round Pond, ME

Winds of Change

The technical winds of change are blowing
I can see it happening every day
Little hand-held boxes with screens aglowing
Thumbs poking in an unusual way.

I truly don't know what to make of it
The electronic world setting the pace
Cell phones are the worst, giving me a fit
I prefer talking to a real live face

No use in my complaining though
I'm just to old for it I guess
I'll feel the wind wherever I go
But rest assured I'll have my GPS

Suzanne Collins
Sedona, AZ

Desert Yearning

Remembering the sea
I drive to a little lake
But it's not the same
There's no pine tree scent
No shores of Maine.

No sound of surf
Relentless and sure
Pounding on the beach—
No surge of tide
Creeping up the beach.

I want to see the sun
Rising on the waves
The moon at midnight
Gleaming on the rocks—
Oh Pine Tree State—
Oh Maine!

Justin Maseychik
Northport, ME

Stag

As I went out tonight to see,
To breathe the deepest greenery
I startled you and saw the flag

Of your great white fear, a stag!
Abruptly running from my green
The edge of quilted meadows,

Lo, behold your ancient sigh,
The huffing of your whole heart
And the pounding part by part,

"I breathe the same air as thee!"
Frightened deer, we both are free
To choose our flight or destiny.

***

Helen Rivas-Rose
Kennebunk, ME

Will You Be My Valentine

Time, you silly thing, I can't see you, can't hear you,
    can barely define you.
Yet, I sure can feel you and I know you're around.
I often think in terms of you, short periods, longer ones,
    and even whole, whole years of you.
You allow me breath and a road to travel on.
So Time, will you be my Valentine?

P. C. Moorehead
North Lake, WI

Room

I add a leaf.
The tiny table expands.

I add another.
It expands more.

It is with my life.

I add a leaf.
I add another.

The seating grows.
There is room for more.

*****

A Moment Here

The flowers are lovely,
a little joy.
That is what I have:
a moment here,
a moment there,
a little joy,
a larger life.

Adele Clark D'Alessandro
Celebration, FL

Cyberspace Baby Shower

"You're not going to be able to do it. Give it up." My husband, Tony hit me in the face with HIS reality. I desperately wanted to arrange a shower for our sixth grandchild. I didn't want to hear his negativity. I wanted the impossible, a face to face conventional baby shower.

My son and his wife surprised us at Christmas with the news that they were going to have their first baby. Paul was forty and Sarah thirty-eight. We had just about given up any hope for more grandchildren. After all, Paul's siblings provided us with five beautiful offspring, ranging in age from two to sixteen. We weren't going to be greedy.

They handed me a dual photo as my gift. It was obviously some kind of sonogram on the one side and a photo of Bugsy, their dog, on the other. I thought, "Could this possibly be a new dog?" We had just lost our family pet of ten years, Siggy. Paul had found him roaming the streets of Washington, D.C. and had given him to us after an extensive search for his owner proved futile. My first thought was that another puppy was in the oven. Then my other daughter-in law Adrianna interrupted, "Come on, can't you see, Paul and Sarah are having a baby." I was dumbfounded, excited and yes, ecstatic. The baby, a girl, was due the end of June.

We found out subsequently, that Sarah's was a high risk pregnancy due to age and some other medical factors. During her visit, we experienced a slight scare, followed by a late night visit to the local hospital. Thank God, everything was fine.

Shortly after the holidays, my daughter Mary-Kim suggested that we host a shower for Sarah. At first, I was eager to start planning, but then I realized that Sarah and Paul lived in San Francisco and to drag her back across the country for a shower was not only impractical, but also risky. Her friends and relatives lived all over the country, including New

Adele Clark D'Alessandro
Celebration, FL

York, Florida, Pennsylvania, Tennessee, New Jersey, Ohio, South Carolina, Virginia and New Mexico. Very few would be able to travel such a great distance to the city by the bay.

I decided that the only solution was to plan a video type conference. I was familiar with the set up since I'd worked for decades as a technical consultant for a major telecommunications company. I just didn't know what facilities were available to residential customers. I started with my computer and found a few sites that offered video calling. My son Paul and I played with the web-cam and found several possibilities, however, the amount of people that could be on the same call was limited. All those involved would have to own a web cam and be familiar with its use. What I wanted to accomplish was the ability to watch Sarah open her gifts and to interact with the senders as simply as possible. I checked the Internet and found several companies that would sell us bandwidth for a live web cast. I even signed up with one company, but was disappointed with their product. The screen would freeze up and you would have to log on again. Also, there was about a thirty second delay from the live view.

We finally came upon a site called <u>live stream .com</u>. It did the trick and it was totally cost free. We were able to send a link to anyone and they could view Paul's production live. He could speak to them but if they wanted to respond, they could join the chat room by setting up a login and password in a matter of seconds. We knew that we could plan a conference call, but that again would involve instructions for the shower attendees. So we decided that as Sarah opened her presents, Paul would call the sender on the phone. The only thing the viewer would have to do would be to turn down the volume on his computer to avoid feedback. We were ready. We had several trial runs until we were satisfied with the view and the volume. I sent invitations via snail mail with the link to the shower. I also followed up with an e-mail including a link to the website.

Adele Clark D'Alessandro
Celebration, FL

Now for the fun.

Paul decorated his living room with balloons and streamers. He put out all the gifts that were delivered to his home. It looked like a genuine baby shower. During the broadcast, I developed a group e-mail. Then I wrote a letter thanking everyone for attending our virtual shower and asking if they wanted some virtual refreshments. I cut and pasted pictures of wine, beer, soda, chips, dinner and desserts, etc. Another e-mail was sent after the viewing. It included party favors found by doing a search for virtual gifts on the internet. In addition, I put two games together for the attendees. For one, I filled a baby bottle with chocolate candy and they were asked to guess the correct number. For the other, I filled a pretty basket with all kinds of baby products and the one who guessed closest to the exact price, won. They were encouraged to guess the answers in the chat room or to call me with their responses. The winners were sent beautiful rose bouquets the next day.

The shower went better than expected. Paul is a bit of a clown so it was very entertaining. Everyone was able to join us by a simple click on a link. Some people entered the site early to create a login for the chat room. Sarah's grandmother was so impressed by the event, and she wanted to know if there was a recording of it. The site does allow you to record the event, but we didn't turn that feature on. The whole shower lasted ninety minutes and most of the 18 logged on stayed with us the entire time. The chatter was continuous. As a memento, we printed a transcript of the chat room.

I was so happy that we were able to succeed in hosting such a long distance shower. What seemed like an impossible dream, turned into an easily attainable reality with help from the Internet. Many families and friends are separated by thousands of miles these days. This was the perfect cyber solution for us and I'm sure it can be for others as well.

Adele Clark D'Alessandro
Celebration, FL

Total cost:
Invitations $129.26
Flowers (prizes) $ 67.00
Prizes $ 54.00

***

Tammy L.R. Meserve
Edgecomb, ME

Monhegan

Ode to an island, mysterious and fair
Boasting of Cathedral woods and fairy houses rare
Blessed is this place of rocky shores and winding trails
A quaint one room schoolhouse
A tiny chapel where "Jesus never fails."
Of white sails and ships, of faraway shores
Of orange monarchs, of simple beauty defined
Of peacefulness and all that is lovely
An inspiration to the heart and to the mind.
A treasure trove of gifts to the spirit,
The Creative Muse makes this island its home
Here it knows freedom to wander
To fulfill, to entice and to roam.
The natives understand a unique existence,
Nearly twelve miles out into the sea
Once you've experienced Monhegan
It will forever tug upon the heartstrings of thee!

Goose River Anthology, 2012//170

Cheryl Wolfe
Delavan, WI

The Plan

Thanksgiving dinner is barely over
and already Grandma is asking everyone
for their Christmas gift list.
Grandma believed in
Black Friday
before it was even invented.
The plan was
To buy the gifts
the day after Thanksgiving
so the month of December
could be spent
snug in the cottage
wrapping gifts
addressing cards
drinking hot cocoa
and watching the snow.

***

Summer Celebration

The leaves sway
in the gentle breeze,
dancing with the sunlight.
As they sway and dip,
they call me
to join them in their
fleeting summer
celebration.

T.A. Cullen
Madison, WI

Story Lines

In my line of sight
face down in the lawn
a deliberately dismantled spinning wheel
discarded glove
and a rain stained letter
drying in the sun.

A tangled fish line
holds a smoke wreathed fisherman transfixed
his fingers tugging to unwind
a hook snagged in weeds
he pulls and tugs
cuts and discards
a glistening web
a snapshot of a bad cast,
and all that went wrong.

***

Maude Olsen
South Bristol, ME

Rotation

The slanting light moves on
    chasing the shadows
    across the wall.
Dusk follows,
    dragging Night behind him.
Another Day
    is on its way to tomorrow.

Irene Zimmerman
Milwaukee, WI

In the Springtime of Her Dying

She held the reins slack in her hands,
letting her pony choose the way.
Unsure at first, it browsed on new clover,
looking back at her now and then, waiting
for direction. When none came, the pony snorted,
tossed its head, sent a shiver down its flanks,
began to trot, then took off in a gallop.

Its mane whipped her face, bringing tears.
Now, where no one could see, she gave
free rein to the fact of her dying—*Inoperable*
the doctor had said. *Maybe five to six months,*
he had answered, reluctantly. She felt the pony's
power beneath her, pumping energy into her heart
and lungs, into the veins and arteries of her spirit.

At the field's edge, the pony slowed to a trot
alongside the row of stones. She thought of
Robert Frost and his springtime chore
of mending walls with his curmudgeon neighbor.
No fence, she knew, would be good enough
to keep out this intruder. She sat up straight,
resolved to move with dignity into the rest of her life.

Sally Woolf-Wade
New Harbor, ME

North Haven Autumn

At last the rusticating folks have gone.
The tennis nets are stored away somewhere.
No mowers hum along the sweeping lawns,
no sails drift down the empty Thorofare.

But lobster boats appear at morning light.
Old trucks emerge—no plates and worn-out treads.
Men check all doors and windows, sealed up tight.
No gardeners tend the faded flower beds.

The daily pace of living gradually slowed,
it's back to quilts and needles, hammers, nails,
to greeting friends on walks along the road,
to kitchen coffee laced with inside tales.

The tools and toys of summer stored on shelves,
the island families now have lives, themselves.

Charles Boldreghini
Collierville, TN

The Best Laid Plans . . .

When Grandfather Angelo Gatti uprooted his family from the close confines of the immigrant settlement near downtown Memphis where they'd lived since 1905, he had something other than more family space in mind. He wanted more of the good things in life, not only for himself, but for Grandmother Maria Teresa and the five children: Lena, 18; Pete, 16, Joe, 14; Louise, 12; and Albert, 10.

The year was 1920. Prohibition had been ratified the year before. Bootleg liquor was flowing freely into the U.S. from Canada and Mexico. Speakeasies, and by the bottle bootleggers, were doing a booming business.

Grandfather Gatti saw this as an opportunity for his family to rise up in the world. He put his small grocery store in the immigrant settlement up for sale and went looking for a place to set the family up in the retail end of the bootleg liquor trade. South of Memphis, at 266 West Mallory, he found it.

The family's new home was a rectangular two-story brick with a screened sleeping porch across the second floor front and a one story clapboard addition at the rear that housed the kitchen. A country store occupied the front half of the first floor. The rear half of that floor served as the family combination living and dining room. Access to the second floor which was made up of a long hall, five bedrooms and the sleeping porch was gained by way of a stairwell on one side of the combo living and dining room.

The outbuildings at the rear of the house included a large wash shed for doing family laundry, a coal shed, a big henhouse and an outhouse. The chicken yard was fenced as was a large garden plot.

The store's front abutted Mallory to the south. A half mile to the west, Mallory entered Riverside Park. The eastern leg of Mallory ran through the community then known as South

Charles Boldreghini
Collierville, TN

Memphis, which was a mile up the road from the Gatti family's new home. To the north of the property, two hilltop Negro settlements were bisected by the railroad that ran south from Memphis on down into Mississippi and bordered the Gatti property one hundred and fifty feet away from the house to the west.

Two sawmills with lumberyards were nearby: one directly across Mallory to the south, and the other to the west, on the far side of the railroad. Two Negro tenant farms occupied the land to the south between the saw mill and the Nonconnah Creek levee. A hardwood factory was just a short piece up the road toward South Memphis.

That hodgepodge of a community had everything Grandfather Gatti needed to make a success of the business ventures he had in mind.

The saw mills' and factory payrolls each Saturday provided ready cash for bootleg liquor sales, with customers coming from the South Memphis community as well as the Negro settlements. And the seclusion of the property made for the sort of privacy needed to set up illuminated bocce courts where Italian men from Memphis and the surrounding area could come on Sunday afternoon to play their native game into the wee hours of Monday morning with no worry about neighbors complaining. The sale of wine from the soon-to-be installed Gatti cellar and sandwiches from the Gatti kitchen would be brisk during the games.

With a readymade workforce of two almost grown sons and an eighteen-year-old soon to be son-in-law, Charlie Boldreghini, who was courting Lena at the time of the family move, the work that needed doing to get things underway went quickly.

By the fall of 1920, a secret room had been created in the henhouse by adding a false rear wall behind the chicken roost. This room became the heart of the bootleg liquor operation. There, the fiery white liquid was changed into a colored, salable product in pint and half pint bottles with fancy

Charles Boldreghini
Collierville, TN

labels and lidded corks. Then, as needed, it was moved to a secret place in the store. Sales were well underway before the end of the year.

Before the August, 1921 wedding day of Charlie and Lena, a wine cellar with two barrels of wine fermenting in it had been installed in the rear of the garage. And three illuminated bocce courts had been laid out in a row along the east side of the house. Italian men began playing bocce on the courts that fall.

And thus the Gatti family prospered during the '20's. They dressed well, dined well, entertained guests (mostly Grandmother's nieces and their families) every Sunday, and had two family cars to gad about in. Grandmother began going to Hot Springs, Arkansas each year for the baths. And Grandfather's bankroll grew.

Then, one morning in October toward the end of the '20's, Grandfather, seeking to strengthen his hold on the good life, drove over into Arkansas to close a business deal. An hour or so after he left a rainstorm blew in from the south. Rain came down in torrents.

Along toward noon, the Gatti family received a telephone call from a sheriff's department in Arkansas. There had been an automobile accident. Angelo Gatti was dead.

Details of the accident were sketchy. There were no witnesses. The sheriff's deputy, who was first on the scene, saw it this way: The driver was headed toward Memphis when he lost control of the car during the heavy downpour. The car left the highway, went down the embankment and flipped onto its side when it entered the drainage ditch. The driver was knocked unconscious and thrown from the car. He landed face down in the rain-filled ditch. The coroner had written on his report: Death by drowning.

And so it was that Grandfather's dream of wealth for the Gatti family died with him in that rain-filled ditch beside a highway in east Arkansas. Not long after his death the Great Depression brought lean times to the Gatti family as it did to

Charles Boldreghini
Collierville, TN

most Americans.

Only Uncle Pete clung to a remnant of the dream. I learned about this one afternoon during the few months I lived in Memphis after I was discharged from the navy in 1946. Uncle owned the family property at that time. We were sitting at a table in the rear of the store talking while we downed a few beers.

After we'd talked some about my years in the navy, he got to talking about those affluent days of the '20's. And thus he became my source of most of what I've written about the Gatti family history during those years.

We ended our talk that day with him telling of the events leading up to and including Grandfather's death, facts of which I was already familiar. But at the end he added a twist of his own that I'd never heard before.

He firmly believed that somewhere in Arkansas there was a piece of property that belonged to the Gatti family. He knew Grandfather had a wad of money on him when he left that morning. And since he was headed home when the accident happened, but no money was found at the scene, that meant he'd closed the deal even though no proof of purchase was found on Grandfather.

"Back then, if you knew a man, many a deal was sealed with a handshake and the paperwork done later in town." Uncle said.

"So you think the guy Nonno made the deal with just kept quiet when he heard about the accident?" I said.

"The dirty skunk kept the money and the property."

"And you've got no idea who or where?"

Uncle shook his head. "All I knew was that Papa was looking to buy another place. Earlier in the year, he took a couple of trips over into Arkansas, and every once in a while after that when he'd had a few too many, he'd run on about buying a booze joint somewhere and adding a gambling joint and a whore house to it. 'Then we'd make some real dough,' he'd say."

Charles Boldreghini
Collierville, TN

Uncle paused thoughtfully, and then took a long swig of beer before he went on. "A couple of months after the accident when I'd had time to think about it some, I made half a dozen trips over into Arkansas. I checked out every backwoods booze joint within fifty miles of Memphis. Nobody would admit to knowing a man named Gatti."

Uncle Pete died in the '50's and the property went to his wife Agnes, who later sold it.

Today all who had any actual memory of the Gatti family history during the '20's are gone. Only hearsay, among those of us who are descendents of the Gatti children, remains.

Of the property itself, nothing remains, except a weed grown acre of land that seems to belie the fact that here, once upon a time, an Italian immigrant family almost saw their dream of wealth in America come true.

***

Avery Allen
Little Rock, AR

Water for Me

Can't you see with your eyes?
And touch with your skin
Apparently, you can't taste
What I taste
Tongue parched for those vile words I've spoken
And tongue quenching for truth, it's always lies
Water for me like the flowers
Water for me like storms
Water for me whether cool or warm
Water for me

Celine Rose Mariotti
Shelton, CT

the immigrants

so often our history books,
speak so little of their contribution,
their sacrifice is often overlooked,
they gathered all they owned,
sailed on a ship, crowded,
and most of the way they were sick,
but they made it to their new home,
the first symbol of their new land,
that grand lady in New York Harbor,
the Statue of Liberty welcomed them in her arms,
they were held over for awhile at an island
it is called Ellis Island,
today it is a museum in their honor,
no one can quite comprehend,
the difficulties they encountered,
for they spoke a foreign tongue,
their cultures were diverse,
but here they settled,
in hopes they would find a better life,
but their life here was hard,
they were discriminated upon,
but this they withstood,
they were given the least of jobs,
but this they withstood,
their children spoke the language of their
parents, but soon they learned English,
and so did their parents,
they learned the American ways,
these immigrants loved their new land,
though times were tough, and a Depression was on,
this they withstood,

(continued)

Celine Rose Mariotti
Shelton, CT

many different nationalities lived in
the same neighborhoods
and became friends, and shared their cultures,
their sons went off to war,
to fight on foreign shores,
their parents lit candles,
and prayed for their boys to come home,
some came home in coffins,
some came home with medals,
these immigrants became citizens,
their children always respected them,
and loved them too,
for they knew that Mom and Dad
had left their families behind,
to come to a strange land,
the immigrants always talked about their country
that they left behind,
they never forgot their culture,
and they maintained their language too,
and when their grandchildren were born,
they passed their culture on to them too,
for these were special people,
who really loved this land,
no monument is big enough,
no museum has enough,
to tell the story of these
immigrants,
who gave so much,
and asked for so little,
for they had pride,
and they had courage too,
so many immigrants,
came to our shores,
so many still come,
and that is why we should

(continued)

Celine Rose Mariotti
Shelton, CT

always keep an open door,
for we should always remember,
how much they have to endure,
to come to America,
and make this land their home.

***

Catherine Wang Hsu
Malden, MA

Survivor

Her eyesight was impaired for several days
Until she found her glasses in the laundry

A twenty dollar bill was missing from her wallet
Then she found it in her pocket

The police car was chasing her down
Then she found the stop sign

As rushing tide washed away her sorrow
She found her relief

Sitting next to his empty chair
She then found poetry

Looking out from her window
Then she found lily buds

When raindrops tapping on her shoulders
She found him with her once more

While listening to the whispering wind at night
She found her soul in peace

Norma J. Crosier
New York, NY

My Mother, Myself

"Mother, I've broken up with Tom." It was Labor Day weekend, 1950. I was visiting from New York at our family home in Adams, Massachusetts, and Mother and I were sitting in the living room after lunch. I glanced over her way and saw just the slightest nod. She looked so small against the large couch. I realized how much frailer she was since my last visit in early summer. The cancer treatments did not seem to be helping.

Sharing this news about Tom with my mother was hard. It meant that she was right and I was wrong. She had known better than I who would or would not make an appropriate husband for me. I was 29 years old and still felt her influence.

I thought back over the years, growing up in this small New England town. My mother set the tone of our household —warm and loving, but with a strong sense of propriety and reserve. I remember her telling a friend one day that we had never had any unpleasantness in our home. I thought that must be a slight exaggeration, but in her eyes it was a fact. We were definitely not wealthy, but she loved adding a touch of elegance whenever she could. The front hallway was the "foyer," the curtains between the hallway and living room were "portieres," the chest of drawers upstairs was a "chiffonier."

My dad was a self-made man, well liked and respected by everyone. He had a promising career at the local bank, but when a teenager, he had to drop out of high school and get a job to support his widowed mother. Perhaps that is why my mother felt such a strong need to set the kind of standards she had grown up with as the daughter of the superintendent of the local woolen mills. And she wanted the best for her three daughters. It was important that we join the local country club and learn to play golf. We would all have a col-

Norma J. Crosier
New York, NY

lege education. My sisters seemed to fall into this pattern easily. I was the youngest and more independent with a mind of my own. Most of my friends did not belong to the country club and their parents did not socialize with my parents. And I fell in love with Tom Harrigan, who would turn out to not quite meet the "necessary requirements."

Tom and I had practically grown up together during our summer vacations at Windsor Pond not far from my home town. My family had a cottage on a hill overlooking the lake and Tom's folks ran the food and beverage concession at the beach. I was good friends with Tom's three sisters and gradually Tom and I began to have stronger feelings towards each other.

Tom was not handsome, but had a kind of casual charm and rugged good looks that I found irresistible. I loved that he would often "one-arm drive" and I would cuddle up in the comfort of his other arm around my shoulder. I felt warm and protected, and in love.

I dutifully followed in my sisters' footsteps at Skidmore College; then, following graduation, I went on to my real goal in life, a job in New York City. We were in the midst of World War II and Tom had been drafted and was serving in the army in the South Pacific. Through our many letters, our feelings for each other continued to grow. Then, after the war he settled back down in his hometown of Springfield, Massachusetts.

By now I had a wonderful life going in New York. The city was exciting, sophisticated, and the center of the world. I had a job in the sales department of American Airlines that I loved, an apartment in Greenwich Village with three roommates, and some good friends.

When I visited Tom in Springfield on weekends, we had our usual wonderful times together, double dating with his friends, and often dancing away the evenings. We soon began thinking about marriage. I felt I loved him as much as ever, but something was not quite right. For one thing, although

Norma J. Crosier
New York, NY

Tom made an effort to be a part of my city life when he visited, he seemed never completely at ease with my friends or the setting.

I remember one specific weekend, when we spent an evening on the town with my roommates and their dates, some still in their officers' uniforms. I couldn't help but feel that Tom, who never went beyond corporal, wasn't quite measuring up, and sensed that, proud as he was, he felt uncomfortable too. Some time after that, he made it clear to me that he would never want to live in New York. I, on the other hand, felt pretty sure I wouldn't want to be anywhere else. I had moved on with my life, while Tom wanted nothing more than to get back to his former one.

One day Tom decided to stop by to visit my mother and "get her blessings" about our plans to marry. Normally it would have been more appropriate to talk with my father, but my dad could often have an off-putting gruff exterior, so Tom felt more comfortable with my mother. I learned later from Tom that she had reacted by bursting into tears. He was so taken by surprise, he couldn't do anything but make an excuse to leave. I was shocked too, and mortified.

"Oh my gosh, Tom, tell me exactly what happened?" I found it hard to believe that my mother, always so composed, had burst into tears.

"Well, she came to the door, looked a little surprised to see me, then invited me in. We sat in the living room and she asked about my family, just talking casually, and then I told her about our plans. That's when she began crying."

"Oh, wow! What did you do then?"

"I didn't know what to do. I sort of apologized, and said I should get going."

I was still baffled. Why had Mother reacted that way? She had never said anything against Tom before. But then I hadn't shared with her how serious we were about each other.

As I thought more about it, I began my own appraisal of

Norma J. Crosier
New York, NY

Tom, while imagining the qualities that Mother might feel strongly about—one, he was of a lower social class, and two, he was a Catholic. Okay, both true, but neither of those reasons was important to me. However, if I were to be completely honest with myself, and Mother might have made this number three, he did tend to be a plodder, not overly ambitious, and only half-hearted about pursuing a college degree.

The unfortunate part is, Mother and I were never able to talk about Tom's visit that day, and discuss what it was that made her so unhappy. It was as if it had never happened— a sure way to "avoid any unpleasantness."

In the end, it was my decision to call it quits with Tom. New York had spoiled me and I knew instinctively that I would be miserable in provincial Springfield. Helping Tom start his own business, which at the moment was running a Laundromat, sounded to me like the end of the world!

Still, I couldn't stop thinking about the role Mother had played. The decision had been not just mine. It was also hers. I had grown up constantly at odds with my mother's standards. And yet, here we were, finally in agreement. I was my mother's daughter after all.

***

Now, sitting here with Mother, I could see how easily she tired. I crossed the room and helped her to her feet, and gently led her upstairs for an afternoon nap.

Maureen Anaya
Berwick, ME

The Musician

The musician traveled from town to town,
His musical notes were a comforting sound.

Both old and young gathered at the city square,
To see the musician fiddling there,
The sick and the lame came out at noon,
To hear the musician playing a tune.

The musician traveled from town to town,
His musical notes were a comforting sound.

He played other instruments of choice,
Sometimes he joined in with his voice.
And encouraged others to join him in song,
A happy crowd would sing along.

The musician traveled from town to town,
His musical notes were a comforting sound.

Spirits would lift at the notes he would play,
He brought happiness to others for another day.
The songs he wrote would be a sign,
A great musician is gift to mankind.

The musician stopped traveling from town to town,
Now only his ghostly music would be a comforting sound.

Naya Clifford
Troy, ME

Two Worlds

Bright wind caught my breath in strong hands as
I rounded my shoulders against the push of snow,
driven across sidewalks, cold car hoods, vacant lots that
stare at me.

Their abandoned husks a shadow of my own ache in
the space you left, unturned covers on that side of the bed.

The wind on your side of the world whips a raspy
lizard tongue, biting sand churns pieces of bombed souls,
        cars, ash
and shattered plans of politicians, businesses, dreams of
        nations, all chaff and rubble.

The rustle of dried leaves filled your eyes when you were
Here for your two week leave, your mind still there
driving armored vehicles, thinking about every bend, every
inch of road, each mound of dirt a potential explosion, a
        potential ending.

Your easy to laugh smile, roughened at the edges, chiseled,
held in check as you hid carefully behind a curtain of duty;
        yet whispered
in an honest way about how impossible it all looked, that
        you needed to
"be there for the guys."

As you laced your boots and hugged your children, you
kissed me and said,
"I only have 30 more days. I'll be back in 30 days."

The trees behind our house stood in silent formation.
Their leafless limbs, waved in the pale winter sky.
Your brown eyes ran full of crushed oak leaves, and acorns,
wrestling with sand.

Miranda Meade
Randolph, NJ

An Ancient Family Portrait

I found the portrait wedged in between two cardboard boxes in the basement.

The picture was singed around the edges, the image faded and musty. I use my thumb to brush away a layer of dust that has settled over the picture, making it impossible to see the details of the people in the portrait. Then I blow on it, a dust cloud billowing up in Sayde's face. Oops.

"Ew!" she squeals, swatting at the dust particles I accidently blew in her face. She glares at me, dust sticking in her eyelashes and her lip gloss and to a few strands of her curly blonde hair.

"Sorry," I mutter.

"Don't waste your breath on insincere apologies; I know you are always looking for ways to annoy me," Sayde snaps, looking back down at the box she's rummaging through. I roll my eyes. Sayde was one for random accusations and I really should have learned by now to just ignore her. I mean really, after a year of the two of us doing nothing but arguing and going at each other's throats, I should know to leave her alone. But for some reason, I just can't. Competing with Sayde has now become one of my best-loved hobbies. I've always been one for playful bantering, ever since this boy in my sixth grade class made fun of my two different colored eyes, I viewed his ignorance as a challenge and since then, I've never backed down. And I've always won. But Sayde is a whole new story. Sayde's been my foul-tempered target ever since she pushed me into a thorn bush and made me sprain my ankle. And no, I'm not exaggerating. She really did that to me. I'm just not the kind of person that takes crap from people, Sayde, or anyone else.

I lower my gaze back to the picture: the grayish and white, grumpy looking couple, the dark-haired teenager, the little girl with pale eyes and a heart-shaped locket around

Miranda Meade
Randolph, NJ

her neck. I study the picture, ignoring the loud crash Sayde makes as she knocks over a box from the top shelf against the wall and it smashes on the floor. Being around Sayde, I've gotten used to crashes.

"Look what I found," Sayde says. I jump, instinctively lowering the picture to keep her from seeing it. It wasn't worth the risk of either getting made fun of or getting the picture snatched from my hands in Sayde's desperate attempt to blame me for something, which is just stupid. But yet again, that's Sayde.

When I look up, Sayde's dangling a heart-shaped locket between two fingers. My eyes widen; it matches the exact necklace the girl's wearing in the picture. I stare at it, gaping at the slightly rusted gold chain and pendant that even looks like it's from 200 years ago.

"You look like a fish." Sayde scrunches up her nose. "Why are you staring like that? It's just a necklace." She tosses it away over her shoulder and continues searching through another box. The clink of the metal hitting the cement floor echoes around the room. I hurry over and scoop up the necklace, running a finger gently over the front of the gold heart. There are small crystals embedded around the edge. I shove it in my pocket to prevent Sayde from seeing it and, after studying it one more time, slip the portrait in after it.

I glance up quickly. Against the wall across from me is a broken mirror, shattered as though someone had thrown something heavy at it from some frustrating event that's now long forgotten. Something stirs in the glass, like fog. Narrowing my eyes, I study it harder.

I gasp. In the mirror in front of me is a faded reflection of the pale-eyed girl, locket-less, her outline hanging like mist in the dust-dappled mirror, her arm extended as though reaching towards me.

And somehow, I know, she's reaching for her locket.

Russell Crabtree
Manchester, ME

Miss Sperling, Kindergarten Teacher

I remember little of what was taught, but the teachers left an indelible impression of what they were as people. I even recall the name of my kindergarten teacher, Miss Sperling. I don't remember a thing she taught, but I will never forget her. She loved us and loved what she was doing.

She very nearly died in a car crash. I saw the other teachers weeping while talking about her. I understood that I would never see her as a teacher again and felt the loss deeply.

My mother and I encountered her years later. The accident had changed her. Miss Sperling insisted on trying to remember my name and I watched as she struggled to recall what had been taken from her. What hadn't changed was her love for children and the message that I was precious to her. She embraced me, holding me with her eyes closed for several minutes. I returned that embrace because I loved her. No machine or technological miracle of distance learning can ever substitute for such an experience. Miss Sperling's gift was herself. What she was crossed six decades to touch me in the here and now.

George Wentz
Sturgeon Bay, WI

Alone on a Rainy Day

It's a melancholy day,
dim and dreary.
Rain falls steadily,
ringlets in puddles of water.

Raindrops roll down the wet glass
bending trees through the blurry window,
as the random rhythm of rain
pecks away at the roof above me.

The mood invites my mind to nostalgia
to recall the sunshine missing from today,
a comfortable place in the past
far from these tears falling from the clouds.

But there is no warmth left
in those dusty attic trunks,
the ones that hold the scent and feel
of clothes packed away long ago.

They can't be filled with those who wore them
to talk, and laugh, and share this day.
The rain is my companion now,
alone—the rain and me.

Jean A. Frame
Glenmoore, PA

Mom's Memories

My playmates and I, six or eight of us, left our homes to play in the fields. Sometimes the girls would bring their doll coaches; sometimes the boys brought hats. We would dig up potatoes and played under the blue sky. We found ripe pears on the ground, a gift from the tree next to a deserted house.

We would have picnics in the fields of wildflowers; sometimes we would play "Marry Me." We made garlands from the wildflowers: buttercup, cornflower, poppy and so many more. The boys would put the garlands in the girls' hair, then one of the boys would be the preacher. The rest of us stood before the "preacher" and he would "marry" us. The same boy always picked me.

We celebrated our childhood in the fields: running, laughing, pushing our doll coaches when we brought them. I look back fondly at my childhood; we did not have any fears.

Eventually, of course, I grew up, as my playmates did. I "left" the boy who always picked me to "marry" him, and I think of him fondly. A new man came into my life many years later and I married him for real. I had two children with him, and now he has passed on.

My children are grown and I have one grandchild. He loves to play outside; he does not have the wide open spaces I had, though. But he can run and play under the blue sky.

As I wind down I savor the memories of my childhood more and more; I am happy to have had such an idyllic childhood.

Thomas C. Collins
New Harbor, ME

Daily Miracles

Into my ninth decade,
and conscious of life's
preciousness, I strive
to use each daily second well.
There are 866,400 of them—
each a miracle of Creation
immediately consumed.

Of all these miracles,
two provide particular joy—
the second I go to bed
and the second I get up.

***

Lifespan

Aging is effortless,
and so is death.

No telling how long
I'll be here.

Mother died at 44,
Aunt Nedra at 101,
their grandfather at 103.

Me? Who knows?
I'm an optimist
and will be 'til I'm not.

Rose Gill
Jackson, NH

Falling Horizontal

Odelia was staring out the window, wanting nothing more than to get out of the car. It was all just so tedious: the car, the drive, life, everything.

"Damn, I hate getting stuck behind big trucks," said Ria. Odelia glanced over at her scowling twin, before going back to looking out the window. Nothing particularly interesting. Maybe an accident would happen, spice up her life a bit. "What's with those rods, anyways?"

Looking at the truck in front of them, Odelia couldn't help but feel like something was going to happen. Big trucks always made her feel like that, no matter what they were carrying. They always looked about ready to tip over. As Odelia stared at the truck, she noted that a few of the rods looked ready to slide off. Why was everything in her life so precarious?

"Ria, don't you think you're driving a little close to the truck?

"Whatever, Odelia. Maybe he'll notice and speed up a bit." There was just no helping it with Ria; she was always so impatient, especially when she was driving. She turned her attention back to the truck, in time to see two rods slide off the back, followed by several more. Ria swore, and swerved to avoid the flying rods, as one flew straight at their windshield. There was a brief moment of excitement and a racing heart, and then everything went black.

The only things Odelia was aware of were the sharp sounds of sirens growing ever closer and of people screaming, hysterical over what they saw; the acrid smells of smoke and burning rubber; and the sight of legs covered in a beautiful ruby red, all blurry. She couldn't seem to move her head, and look away from that lovely red. She closed her eyes, ready for whatever might happen next. With her eyes closed, she got the sensation that she was falling away from

Rose Gill
Jackson, NH

everything, falling horizontally. She could tell she wasn't fly-ing, because there was a certain lack of any control. She was hurtling along across the landscape and the earth had just been tipped on its side.

She opened her eyes again and saw events and people and landscapes rushing past her, as if she were still with Ria in the car, driving down the highway. She thought she wouldn't mind floating here forever, moving along at whatev-er pace took her, always going somewhere, never sure where. Odelia smiled, at nothing, at everything, and she let her body relax, let it melt into the air and then, for the first time she could ever remember, she felt like she truly existed.

***

Patricia Janke
Wauwatosa, WI

My Picture Window

My picture-window shows
Frosted branches
Bleached-soft snow
Subdued light caches

This chilly desert winter
Nears its demise
My picture window captures
Mother-nature's surprise
Slides of winter prints
Framed in time to show
Every season's art
Through
My picture window

Janet Morgan
Wiscasset, ME

Early Morning Adventure

It was still dark that morning, but I was up early because this was to be a very special day. I leapt from beneath my warm covers, turned on my bedside light, and crossed to my bureau. I dressed in layers so I would be able to peel some off should it become too warm later that day. Once dressed, I opened my bedroom door, shut off the light, and fairly bounced towards the staircase.

I could hear my mother moving around in the kitchen below. I knew she was packing breakfast for Dad and me. *A large thermos of coffee, a smaller one of milk, and something to eat,* I thought, as the dim light radiating from the kitchen lit my way down the stairs. I detoured into the bathroom to retrieve my outer gear: a heavy jacket, ski pants, boots, scarf, hat, and two pairs of mittens. Two pairs because we were going to a place where I would need to keep taking my mittens on and off throughout the day and I was liable to lose at least one.

By the time I heard my father's footsteps on the stairs, I was ready. I followed him into the kitchen just in time to see my mother put the two thermos jugs and a greasy paper bag into our picnic basket. I didn't have to wonder what was in the bag, for I had watched my parents making donuts the night before. I knew now why I had been allowed just one.

I was about to go on an adventure with my father—just me. It was one of the few things we ever did together—just the two of us. Before long we were in Dad's truck and on our way. What a treat! It was the first time my ten-year-old frame had ever settled into the passenger side of the new-to-us vehicle. I don't remember much about that ride, probably because I dozed off almost as soon as we took off, but I was jerked awake when the truck finally stopped on the side of the road. We had arrived at Damariscotta River, where people were heading out onto the ice.

Janet Morgan
Wiscasset, ME

Dad called out for me to join him as he pulled two buckets and the basket from the truck bed. We stepped off the side of the road where the river came up to meet us. "Come on," Dad said as his long stride and brisk steps left me behind. I couldn't follow him! There was open water in front of me! I stared in horror at the sight of the rising water. I hesitated before bravely walking out onto a series of long boards. Then I stupidly stopped. I began to sink. Cold water was rapidly reaching the top of my rubber boots. "Jump," Dad said as his flashlight lit the next spot I was to venture onto.

I did, but I wasn't much better off because now I was on an ice floe. That, too, was sinking. "You have to jump again, and again, until you get over to me." Dad's calm voice urged me on as he stood on firm ice. Oh, I could see where this was getting me. I was going to drown and no one would ever see me again. I imagined my short life passing before me as I realized that this was why my 5-year-old brother had not been invited to come with us. Dad kept yelling at me and I kept jumping and sinking and jumping and sinking, until I was finally at his side. Pride surged through me as I felt that I had passed some ice fishing rite of passage.

Relief coursed through my body and no thoughts of the return journey entered my mind. Do all children blank out future peril and focus on the thrill of the moment? Well, that's what I did. My mind cleared of all negative thoughts as a cheerful sun rose during our walk past ice shanty after ice shanty.

Dad pointed out his shanty in the distance. He had come out a few days earlier and moved the building onto the ice, along with a stove and all his fishing gear. As we entered the tiny camp, I noticed that the long rectangular hole we'd be fishing from had already been cut. Once Dad had the fire lit, we were ready to fish. Dad cut the worms and slid them onto hooks that hung from the ends of waterproof strings wound around a long, horizontal stick. There were about a dozen lines, but in the beginning I was assigned only one.

Janet Morgan
Wiscasset, ME

Dad showed me how to watch for that certain tug before pulling on my string. The first few times my line jerked up and down, I was too slow. It didn't matter, though, because Dad was fast, very fast. He had caught dozens of smelts before we took a coffee break. I got the milk, of course, but Dad gave me a treat: he added a good dollop of coffee to my drink. What fun it was, to be drinking coffee and eating donuts with my father while we watched the lines slowly sway with the current!

It was the greatest thrill of my life when I pulled in my first smelt. After he demonstrated the art of removing fish from hook, I wanted to bait my own hook before returning it to the water. Dad knew better. I was a klutz and was likely to be sending a piece of my finger down for the fish to dine on. It was a few more years before he trusted me with worm and hook. For now I was delighted to slip that first smelt into the bucket of wiggling fish.

It was then that I realized something dreadful. These were live creatures and they were *dying.* I glanced over at my father and wondered if we could let them go, but the look he gave me told me to suck it up and say nothing. Tears glistened in my eyes. When I caught my second smelt; however, I was into the catch. I had no further thoughts for the short lives of the poor smelts.

When it was time to leave with our two buckets filled with smelts, an image of the return to shore assailed me. I remembered that I would have to jump back over those ice floes and onto the long boards. Now I knew how pirates felt when they were forced to walk the plank. I was dreading it, but the day had turned sunny and bright. Nothing could go wrong. The tide had turned leaving very little water near the shoreline.

Back home I lorded it over my baby brother. We had returned with a bountiful harvest for neighbors and friends and I had no room in me for sad thoughts over the smelts. They were now considered food and we would be eating them for supper tonight.

Lorelee Sienkowski
Packwaukee, WI

Sunday Phone Calls

"Oh, Gramma!" He wooed, as he jumped on the bed;
I live in the phone in his hand.
"Gramma, you ready?" conspiracy reigned,
And "we" jumped at his every command.

He climbed on the pillow, his tiny knees bent,
Then he jumped to the mattress, his motions all spent.

He jumped and we giggled; he jumped and we laughed.
Then I heard the phone drop and his frightened gasp.

"Oh, Gramma," he worried, "are you still okay?"
"Oh Grandson," I told him, "you've brightened my day."

***

Maude Olsen
South Bristol, ME

Calligrapher's Song

Those dancing letters come and go;
From out of nowhere they appear,
Provoking laughter, or a tear.
While some spell words, some just glow,
And some are fuzzy, others clear.
But whether they will speed right by
Or linger on to catch the eye,
Is anybody's guess, it seems.
They even entertain my dreams,
Till I awake in wonderment
At whence they came and where they went!

Sylvia Little-Sweat
Wingate, NC

Baptismal Font

Together in this church
for more than fifty years
but on this special day
no longer side by side—
he in a wheel chair
in the aisle; she, flanked
by family down the pew.

Years before he had
led all worshiping
hearts—hers too—
but now his heart
is heavy with memory
while hers is adrift
on a forgetful sea.

It is only when he nears
the baptismal font that
she breaches time's reach
and in a flash of knowing
bends to touch his arm
and kiss his face—wordless
as being one once more.

Reggie Marra
Naugatuck, CT

Please Don't Abandon Me

She makes the phone request unsteadily
aware she's stuck and stationary two
years after the divorce, feels impatience
juxtaposed with my genuine support.
Misguided rebound relationship ends
ugly, compounds the seventeen-year loss,
pillcohol cocktails damage head and car,
embarrassed, scared and hurt she tries again.
Po' ho's performance poetry helps her
slam depression eighteen months until a
second rebound gets away, leaving her
defenseless and blind to any exit.
Too sad to talk, she texts, I drive fifty-
two familiar miles to Hiawatha Road.

***

Toni Ortner
Brattleboro, VT

Snowstorm

We almost missed
a small clearing under tall firs
no snow on the ground
steps from clear running water
a square bed of flattened leaves trampled neatly down
bordered by branches and sticks

Deer high up on the bluff watch us
place
sweet red apples on the drifts.

Dwayne Magee
Mechanicsburg, PA

The Communication of the Dead

It was late October. The morning sun was as golden as the foliage of the trees that lined the asphalt driveway of the Silver Spring Presbyterian Church. Mild winds were moving through central Pennsylvania, and the temperatures were at least ten degrees warmer than they should have been. They call it *Indian summer.* Folks have been calling it that for about as long as there has ever been a Silver Spring Presbyterian Church.

As I neared the meeting house where I was to be attending the funeral of a dear friend, I brought my car to a stop adjacent to an old cemetery. In just a few hours there would be one more gravestone, one more marble tree in this forest of arched tributes.

The cemetery was like a small-scale city of odd-shaped buildings, each one competing for the prize of being most ornate. Many of the graves were positioned in such a way so that the headstones were all facing east, towards the rising sun. They were facing me. Their smooth, white facades held a cryptic expression like the stolid gaze of a great white shark. A dilapidated wall surrounded the miniature metropolis. The wall was comprised of thousands of stones, the largest of which sat at the bottom of the section nearest to me. Its engraved markings read "Established 1734."

Behind the wall, I could read some of the names on the headstones. *Harris, Lamb, Trindle...*these were all names I recognized. They were the names of nearby towns and streets. Fisher, Silver, Hoge...I turned off the ignition.

The wind worked its way through the branches of the tall oaks surrounding me and I hypnotically monitored the descent of a single, falling leaf. The air cradled its precious cargo and brought it quietly to the ground before a pair of thin, stark white monuments.

Dwayne Magee
Mechanicsburg, PA

John Carothers, Born 1739 Died 1798
Mary Carothers, Born 1740 Died 1798

Aroused from my beauty of nature induced stupor by the sudden realization of the time, I gathered my things and stepped from the car.

"What do you think of our little memorial?"

The contemptuous voice startled me. An elderly gentleman had been resting near me where part of the outer wall of the cemetery had collapsed. Apparently, I had inadvertently aroused him from his slumber.

"It's old," I pronounced; assuming he was talking to me. "And quiet."

The man's face took on a stern shape of disagreement. I could now see his eyes were bright blue but they seemed to dim as he looked me over.

"I disagree," he stated emphatically. "Sometimes it's so loud here, I can't hear myself think." Then he turned his head to look out over the sea of tombstones. "These graves...there are so many...they never shut up." He shifted his gaze back towards me. "I find it difficult to rest here."

He paused only for a moment and then spoke again.

"You here for the funeral?" he asked.

"Yes," I replied.

He took a few steps towards me and then stopped to pick up a rake, hidden in the tall grass between us. As he spoke, he began tending to the twin monuments of John and Mary Carothers where the leaf had fallen. He was tall and thin. He looked as though he had lived two life times and had forgotten to eat in either one of them. He wore a blue, plaid shirt under an ancient pair of baggy, green overalls. His hair was white.

"Your friend didn't get a very good spot."

"Is that right?"

"They'll bury him back there," he said as he raked and

Dwayne Magee
Mechanicsburg, PA

pointed with his head, "by the highway."

When he finished his raking, he leaned the implement against one of the neighboring markers. Extending an obligatory, lanky appendage towards me, he introduced himself.

"I'm John Carothers." His tone was acrimonious.

I accepted his hand somewhat reservedly as I again read the inscriptions on the monuments where he had been laboring. His skin was cold and milky white. He felt brittle and I let go of him quickly for fear that something might break.

"Nice to meet you," I said. "I'm Walter."

Something was bothering the old man. Seemingly, it was me. His bright blue eyes were on fire.

"I'm not an idiot you know."

"I'm sorry?"

"I know what you are thinking. You are thinking 'Do I go inside now or does this lonely old man need someone to talk to.' Well I'm not lonely and I don't give a damn what you do!"

He was shaking like an old bag of bones. An ugly, sinister smile presented itself upon his wrinkled face revealing an ugly mouthful of gray and yellow teeth.

"It makes no difference to me or anyone else. Go, stay, get in your car and leave...turn right...turn left. Your petty decisions mean *nothing!*"

My tolerance for the man was diminishing at a rate directly proportional to that of his mental faculties.

"We think we're something, don't we? As if the choices we make really matter. Well, they don't! Look around you. Look at all these graves. Go on, look! Do you think any of the decisions these people ever made mean anything now? They're all dead!"

I looked at his wrists for a medical bracelet but he apparently hadn't escaped from anywhere.

"Our choices mean nothing and the sooner you understand that, the better off you'll be."

"Well..." I started to speak but couldn't. I cleared my throat and tried again. "Well, that is umm...certainly one

Dwayne Magee
Mechanicsburg, PA

opinion."

Whatever it was I was *supposed* to say, I apparently hadn't said it. The old man set his narrow shoulders back and looked at me as though I was the one with only half a mind.

"Haven't you heard of us?"

I always make it my habit to allow myself some discomfort when someone I am speaking with starts referring to themselves in the plural form.

"John and Mary Carothers," he pronounced as though hearing the names might somehow help me. "We were poisoned," he added, "by our housemaid, Sarah Clark."

I looked around for a third monument with the name Clark on it.

"She's not here you halfwit!"

"Yes...of course not."

"John and Mary..."

He paused for a moment and knelt to place his hands on one of the tombstones.

"Dear, dear Mary..."

A tear appeared in the corner of his eye. A moment or so passed until he resumed his story.

"We had a son. Sarah was quite fond of him. She loved him. Their feelings, this common housemaid and our son, were mutual. They were in love. But we wanted something better for our son than for him to be married to a lowly servant. So, we forbade it and that is when Sarah hatched her plan. She added arsenic to our butter churn and poisoned us both."

I stared at him in disbelief. I tried to speak but he went on as though I wasn't even there anymore.

"Do you expect me to believe..."

"Mary survived. She didn't realize. Of course, she still persisted in her opposition to the relationship and so Sarah churned a second batch of poisoned butter. This time Mary died but Sarah's crime was discovered and they hanged her for it. In fact, she was the first woman ever hanged in our

Dwayne Magee
Mechanicsburg, PA

county. So you see, all of that love, all of that passion, all of the anger and angst." He clenched his pale fists in front of him and I watched them get whiter. "It was all meaningless!"

I heard him exude a sound that was more animal-like than human.

"Does any of this matter to you?" he snarled.

"Well. Not really."

"Of course it doesn't! That is precisely my point!"

Then, like the schizophrenic I deduced him to be, the old man started taking on the voices of the dead.

"No son of ours will ever marry a low-life like Sarah."

"You'll find someone else, someone more...worthy."

"Oh! But please Master John. Can't you see I love him?"

"Please, Father! I love Sarah. I don't care who she is or what she does. I only know I want to be with her forever."

"Doesn't it sicken you?" The old man was back. "We were all so caught up in ourselves. And now look at us. We're all dead. And we have been dead for two centuries. None of it matters."

An icy, distant stare came over the man's face.

"Look at us now," he repeated in a low voice.

The cemetery grew eerily silent and the tombstones towered above us, taller than the century old oak trees in our midst. The dead were amassing their choir. The warm, autumn breeze hushed itself in reverence and John Carothers spoke his last words on earth before joining them in their sovereign hymn of ultimate jurisdiction.

"What do the dead say to us?" he asked rhetorically, "They say, 'We are dead!' and that is enough!"

Charles W. Van Buren
Brunswick, GA

The Beach at Night

The sound of the rolling surf,
is sweet music to my ear,
if it would not spoil the mood,
I would stand up and cheer.

The moonlight on the rolling sea,
to me is an awesome sight,
I feel as though I've gone to heaven,
when I walk the beach at night.

Sometimes, when I watch the sea,
light flashes as the waves part,
greetings from a lonesome jellyfish,
saying hello to my heart.

Walking along, I can look up,
and see the stars so bright,
they're the beacon to light my way,
when I walk the beach at night.

As I stroll down by the shore,
I get the feel of contentment,
It seems to take away my cares,
and my feelings of resentment.

The breeze blowing across the sand,
seems to make all things seem right,
I'm alone, but I don't care,
when I walk the beach at night.

Jean Biegun
Manitowoc, WI

Winter Salutation

Come winter, I turn to the trees,
to their sure, beckoning branches
lifted to that massive sky:
Look! they chant, *We are here!*

I drive along their highway meditation,
am small audience walking through
forest crescendos. Night folds
on an old thick-bark maple
outside my window and me within
joined in quiet recollection.

Yes, in past seasons they swelled
with work—made the needed air-
giving leaves, harbored remarkable
squabbly spilling nests, and filled
bins and caches with fruit and seed.

But now winter's spareness expects
reflection, the accounting of blessings,
and so I turn to trees for daily lessons
in raising joy-strong limbs
bared to morning's sun: *We are here!*
We are here!

Kimberly K. Thompson
Fairmont, WV

Seasons

Huddled close together like old women gossiping,
stood the trees in the dead woods.
Stripped of their fine green raiment and pillaged
garments of yellow, orange, red and brass,
now just brown, crumbling heaps littering the
embarrassed grass, banished finery of their summer's past.
Their once proud bodies that flowed with
sap and green velvet texture
now shriveled, haggard, brown and empty,
sucked dry by the cruel late fall.
The trees stand solemnly—
waiting for the harsh blast that proclaims...
winter.

***

Veronica Kegel-Giglio
Philadelphia, PA

Blue Times

He made me sad and he made me blue.
That's why I am talking to you. Do you think we're
      through?
He always made me feel like there was more that I should
      do.
So what am I to do?
I've loved him, but now it hurts. That's always the worst.
I want to believe the sun will shine again one day
And happiness can again come my way.
So what can I say, God
When will be the day?

F. Anthony D'Alessandro
Celebration, FL

Show Them You're Not Afraid to Die!

It seems that Rome never stops teaching me lessons. Just when I think I've got a grip on all the city's offerings, it presents me with a new wrinkle. On several different occasions, I've been a fortunate pilgrim in that Eternal City. I've strolled through the pages of its storied history before, and repeatedly toured most of its recommended sites. Surely, I've walked in Nero's footprints, stood where ancient Roman senators chatted, and sat where gladiators collapsed. With each visit, new and intriguing insights revealed themselves.

I've explored with tour groups, and as an individual. Some of the city's more knowledgeable guides personally escorted me around the Eternal City. With all this exposure, I quickly realized that in many ways, Rome reminded me of my birthplace in New York City, across the Big Pond. There, I'd learned the most efficient ways to cross and crisscross Broadway. I suspect Rome's glamorous answer to Broadway is that gilded street called the *Via Veneto.*

Cab drivers seemed similar in both cities. During my latest Roman excursion, I commandeered a cabbie to take me from the Coliseum to my hotel near the *Via Veneto.* After a few dizzying turns, I asked my driver (in Italian) if he'd been a protégé of Magellan. To my surprise a wide, toothy grin covered his face. The driver proceeded to take me on a whirlwind adventure. He crossed traffic lines, cut off other vehicles, wove in the wrong lanes, ran a light or two, and zig zagged countless times. When I finally pleaded for caution, he decided to give me a free lecture. The cabbie said, "This is not like your bad joke about circumnavigating explorers. I'm going to tell you about the history of the wall surrounding parts of Rome." He proved as interesting as any high-priced guide I'd hired. I did make it to the hotel ten minutes ahead of my friends who'd taken the cab ahead of me. I'd spent two fewer Euros as well.

F. Anthony D'Alessandro
Celebration, FL

Based on my experience with this driver, and other Italian drivers of automobiles and motor scooters, Rome made me a wary pedestrian. I was as cautious as someone setting his first mousetrap. The following day, a group of us from the same hotel hired a tour professional to walk us through more Roman history. Our guide Angela appeared to live up to the reverence implied by her name. Her soft spoken, sweet, and perhaps even spiritual voice comforted me. I thoroughly enjoyed the first few minutes of our stroll with Angela.

Without realizing it, I'd wandered to the head of our pack. On the street beside us, Roman motorists and cyclists drove like stunt drivers and candidates for the Demolition Derby. I eased into the crosswalk much like a year old child taking his first measured steps. I exhibited little bluster, less confidence, and a willingness to make a quick and decisive retreat. I knew that eventually I had to cross the *Via Veneto*. Fear, actually terror, prevented my taking that first step.

A Federico Fellini moment also captivated me. Suddenly, I stood on *La Dolce Vita's* movie set. After a momentary, mouth agape daydream, I actually placed my shaky right foot on the *Via Veneto*. I gawked at Harry's Bar across the way. I felt disappointed. It seemed that the movie stars moved their parties elsewhere. None of them strolled in that magical place. Without invitation, Angela burst into my daydream and forced me back to reality.

From behind my left ear, Angela's voice chirped. Through a faint smile, she said, "Anthony, this is not a ballet recital. Step out into that *Via Veneto* pavement now. Do it with conviction." Suddenly, I became aware of my heart's existence. It began pounding. Sweat sparkled across my hands. I then rubbed them with a wipe as if scrubbing before a meal.

I giggled as my hands quivered. The group laughed. An unexpected Jeckel and Hyde moment surfaced. Who was this woman? It forced me to wonder if her name represented a misnomer. Angela's lips pursed, her face took on the color of

F. Anthony D'Alessandro
Celebration, FL

an overripe tomato. With a voice rife with impatience, she bellowed as loudly as an opera baritone, "Anthony, step out into that street now. Show them you're not afraid to die!"

I'd seen military drill instructors operate, experienced the wrath of hoarse voiced frustrated football coaches, and been tossed about by the Sister Cruella of my elementary school days. None of them would have motivated me more effectively than Angela. I felt like a virtual knitting needle poked me.

I bolted onto that zebra-striped crosswalk and peeked back furtively. I feared Angela's reprimand. I also sensed that I'd turned into the mother duck and all my baby ducklings tagged along. My fellow tourists followed in my steps. Amazingly, that discordant parade of grumbling and impatient vehicles calmed, stopped, and waited for the entire entourage to cross. Angela shouted, "Bravo!" Wimp that I am, I never turned to acknowledge her words.

Angela continued training me on Roman guerilla street crossing techniques throughout the rest of our tour. She stoked the fires for my newly discovered aggressiveness. I dreaded another of her rants. For the rest of my stay, I employed her street crossing style on a daily basis. I'm still a tad worried about recommending Angela's axiom to all travelers. I do know it worked for me.

When a friend asked, "Will you cross Broadway with a show them you're not afraid to die attitude?" I whispered, "When in Rome...."

Lilli Lee Buck
Bristol, VA

The Last Dance of Marguerite

There marches through the castle hall,
    In beauty rare, the prince's bride.
There comes a surly wedding guest,
    Who clasps her sternly, from the side.

"Will you dance with me, fair Marguerite,
    One last dance before you go,
Although you are the prince's bride?
    Still, I never thought it would be so."

"Tell me that you love me, Willie dear,
    Whisper to me in accents sweet,
That will come as the cooling mists of evening,
    In fields parched by the summer heat."

"I do not love you, Marguerite,
    Nor will I speak in accents sweet,
That will come as the cooling mists of evening,
    In fields parched by the summer heat."

"Tell me that you love me, Willie dear.
    It will be for me the stream of life,
That could sustain me in the desert sand,
    Without water, food, or end of strife."

"I do not love you, Marguerite.
    There will be for you no stream of life,
To sustain you in the desert sand,
    Without water, food, or end of strife."

Lilli Buck
Bristol, VA

"Tell me that you love me, Willie dear.
        I have often prayed on bended knee
That you could forgive my heart's worst folly
        That has caused me to forsaken thee."

"I do not love you, Marguerite.
        Although you pray on bended knee,
I cannot forgive your heart's worst folly,
        That has caused you to forsaken me."

The bagpipes skirl, the dancers whirl,
        And lo! Upon the white
Satin of her wedding dress
        Appears a dark and crimson stripe.

"Tell me that you love me, Willie dear.
        Whisper as the murmuring brooklets flow.
It could cool this fever on my brow,
        And ease this sharp and raging blow."

"I do not love you, Marguerite,
        Neither as the murmuring brooklets flow
Will I cool that fever on your brow,
        Nor ease that sharp and raging blow."

"Tell me that you love me, Willie dear!
        Such words could lift me from my swoon,
And give me back the will to live,
        And heal my heart's sore aching wound."

"I do not love you, Marguerite!
        Nothing can lift you from your swoon.
You do not have the right to live.
        Nothing can heal your heart's sore wound."

Lilli Buck
Bristol, VA

The lady sighed a ragged sigh,
    And she could sigh no more.
In a dizzy swoon of grief and blood,
    She fell upon the castle floor.

"Tell me that you love me, Marguerite,
    For it's now I pray on bended knee,
That you'll forgive this proud and jealous heart
    That has caused me for to murder thee."

"Oh, yes, I love you, Willie dear,
    And I will come and wait for thee,
To join you in the blackest Hell,
    When they hang you from the gallows tree."

They hanged him from the gallows tree,
    And in the mid hour of the night,
There appeared out of the darkness drear
    An image of a lady bright.

"I will always love you, Willie dear,
    But I have lost you for eternity.
For the Savior has come to take me to Heaven,
    Where you, alas, will never be."

Joe Oliver
Poinciana, FL

It Changed My Life

High School was coming to an end, the time June 1965. I gave no thought of what my next step in life would be. One day my friend Mike Lopez said a few innocent words grouped together into a sentence, "Hey want to join the Marine Corps?" What a question, join the Marine Corps?

I was never much of a joiner of anything; well there was the Cub Scouts and Junior Achievement. I really had a good time in both of those endeavors. I figured maybe joining the Marine's would be the same. I mean who doesn't want to join a group and have a good time, right?

Off to meet the recruiters. I can still see them standing ramrod straight in this beautiful uniform. Later I would learn that this beautiful uniform had a name, "Marine Dress Blues!" My first thoughts, remember I was seventeen at the time, was the girls are going to love me in that beautiful uniform!

Being a city kid growing up in a row house in a wonderful Blue Collar neighborhood, I was what you would call a greaser. Back then one was either a Collegiate or a Greaser. I had the DA, black leather jacket, pompadour hairdo, hung on a corner, and well, I was a city kid, and I loved every minute of it. All I could think about was that beautiful uniform.

Of course I should have maybe given the year 1965 and a little country in South East Asia some thought. Hey, forget about the year and some country halfway around the world. My thoughts were of that beautiful uniform and the girls it would attract.

My parents were the only thing standing between me and that beautiful uniform. I was only seventeen and needed their permission to join the Marines.

The recruiter arrived at our home and immediately recognizes my mother was in charge. His presentation was spot on

Joe Oliver
Poinciana, FL

and lasted for forty five minutes. When he finished he asked my mother if she had any questions, she didn't.

My mother turned to my father who had not said a word or asked a question during the presentation and asked, "What do you think?"

My father looked at me and then back to the recruiter and asked, "He (meaning me) is going to look like you in three months?"

The Marine recruiter answered, "Yes, sir, Mr. Oliver!"

My father then asked the recruiter, "Can you take him tonight?"

Semper Fi

***

Patricia Helmberger
Grand Rapids, MN

Turn Reflections in a Canoe

The sky is in the water,
The trees are standing upside down.
We float among the clouds,
Brushing against the trees,
Dipping our paddles among the branches.
A small painted turtle
Slips from its log
Into the bright blue sky,
Disappearing among the pines.
When we reach the shore
The world rights itself:
The sky above,
The trees standing as they should.

Susan Dahlgren Daigneault
N. Berwick, ME

A Love Story

"In Flanders Field, the poppies grow, among the crosses, row on row." Memorial Day, 2006. The poppies this day are of the paper variety, distributed by various veterans' organizations so that we will not forget our veterans. As representatives of these groups drift in and out of Dad's room in the Northern Maine Veteran's Home in Caribou, Maine, I remember earlier Memorial Days proudly watching Dad in our community's parade, waving a paper poppy at him as he marched by. Today, there is no marching. Dad has pneumonia and will not march again.

I have just arrived at his bedside, having driven five hours nonstop from my home in southern Maine. I have not seen Dad since April and am overcome by his frail and feverish state. I take his large, square hand in mine, lean over to kiss his forehead, and bolt for the door, overcome with emotion. I lean against the corridor wall, cover my face with my hands, and sob uncontrollably, sobs that come from the deepest part of my being, that place where love resides. I know that Dad is not going to come home again.

I gain control and return to Dad's room. With family surrounding him, Dad drifts in and out of awareness. His hands are busy, making repetitive movements as if he is sewing the edges of his sheets, needle in through one side, thread over the top, and needle out. Was he back in the days when those strong hands sewed the tags on 100 pound sacks of potatoes, tags that indicated that he had inspected the potatoes for quality and certified that they were sound for next season's seed? Because Dad can't tell us what occupies his thoughts, we will never know for sure what his restlessness is all about.

As the afternoon wears on, Mom wears out. It has been a long day for her, a long winter of bedside watches. Her children are arriving from distances to witness the last act.

Susan Dahlgren Daigneault
N. Berwick, ME

A drama is writing itself and she is not the director. Her control is slipping away and the only decision she can make is whether to stay a while longer or go home. She leaves and I decide to stay with Dad. Before leaving, she warns me about the dangers of moose crossing the roads and hopes that I'll be home before dark. Here is Mom still being Mom, concerned about my safety.

I am alone with Dad and I move into the one cushioned, high-backed chair that is standard feature in hospital rooms. I push the chair close to the bed so that I can hold Dad's hand. My smaller hand rests easily within his larger hand and he responds to my touch. He knows I am with him and I am overcome with contentment. There is nowhere else on this earth that I want to be at that moment. Oh, God, please let this time continue into timelessness....

I hear my dad's faint voice. He is trying to tell me something, and I move even closer, struggling to understand. I can pick out several words: animals, cruelty, people. Has he witnessed some awful cruelty in his lifetime? Later I wonder if he was referring to how we treat animals better than people in that we euthanize our beloved animals when they suffer. Is he telling me about his own suffering? If so, I am powerless to provide relief. I can only continue to love him, to hold his hand, to bear witness to this last chapter.

We nap for a time, I in the chair and Dad in his bed. Even in sleep, I hold onto his dry, feverish hand, unwilling to break this connection. Supper comes. Vegetable soup, milk, a tuna sandwich. "Would you like some soup, Dad?" A nod. I pull the tray over closer to his bed and sit on the edge. I scoop up a small spoonful of soup and offer it to him. He opens wide and takes the broth. He chews the carrot pieces. I give him another spoonful and then he motions that he has had enough. He points toward the napkin on his tray and I hold it to his mouth to receive the carrots that he is not able to swallow. He slumps back down on his pillow, exhausted from this effort of eating, and I move the tray away.

Susan Dahlgren Daigneault
N. Berwick, ME

I settle back in my chair and again take Dad's hand, memorizing the shape and texture. Square hands, hands that could lift hundred pound sacks of potatoes all day long and still have strength enough to sweep up the floors before quitting for the night. Hands that picked me up off the ground, knees full of gravel and bleeding, having fallen from my bike on my first try riding a two-wheeler. Hands that held my son on his baptismal day. Hands that restlessly tapped out a cadence on the kitchen table: one, two, three, four...one, two, three, four, five. Hands that fed me when I was a baby....

And I remember and drift back to those early days when I sit in my highchair, my squirmy, dimpled self, anticipating a supper of strained carrots and applesauce. "Da Da Da Da" He mixes the Gerber carrots around in the bowl, teasing me. "Smile, Susie. Show me that new tooth." I smile from ear to ear, drooling out of both sides of my mouth, unable to contain my joy. Blue eyes meet blue eyes and I am in love, a love that will be one of the most profound in my life.

Then he fed me and today I repeat the ritual. It is what I can do for him. As night creeps in, its blanket of darkness covering this day, I hear the nurses making their rounds, preparing the patients for bed. When Dad's nurse comes by, she assures me that Dad will rest comfortably, that he will have medication to help him sleep and to relieve pain. I kiss my dad, ready to take my leave before the Aroostook County moose start to patrol the highways. "I love you, Dad. I'll see you in the morning. Have a good night's sleep." How many times have Dad and I offered each other this same goodnight? Simple words, our private ritual.

I reluctantly let go of his hand. As I walk from his room, I look back once, twice, three times, saying my silent prayer. Please, God, watch over him tonight.

Memorial Day is ending. "In Flanders Fields[1], the poppies grow..."

When I return to Dad's side the next day, I instinctively

Susan Dahlgren Daigneault
N. Berwick, ME

know that I will not leave until this struggle is over. At 10:30 that evening, May 31st, surrounded by his loving family, our dad went home. We lost a beloved father and our country lost a true American hero. Dad was Lt. Edward C. Dahlgren, one of Maine's few Medal of Honor recipients. What he had to do in World War II, no man should have to do. His courageous actions throughout his service, his leadership, and his love for family and his community in Northern Maine remain a lasting legacy of a man who simply did his duty.

[1]"In Flanders Field" by Col. John McCrea, May, 1915.

***

Karen Lewis Foley
Topsham, ME

After Waking

A scrap of half-recalled dream
flutters into your field
of memory and out
like a tatter from a prayer flag
left in the wind
to be carried many places
for it has no root
but this piece of dream does
and it grows deep

GOOSE RIVER ANTHOLOGY, 2013

We seek selections of fine poetry, essays, and short stories (3,000 words or less) for the 11th annual *Goose River Anthology, 2013*. The book will be beautifully produced with full color cover and hard covers will have a full color dust jacket.

You may submit even if you have been published before in a previous edition of the *Goose River Anthology*. We retain one-time publishing rights. All rights revert back to the author after publication. You may submit as many pieces as you like.

EARN CASH ROYALTIES. Author will receive a 10% royalty on all sales that he or she generates.

There is no purchase required and nothing is required of the author for publication. Deadline for submissions is March 31, 2013. Publication will be in the fall of 2013 (they make great Christmas gifts). Guidelines are as follows:

- Submit clean, typed copy—mandatory
- E mail a Word or Word Perfect file to us (if possible)
- Reading fee: $1.00 per page
- Do not put two poems on the same page
- Essays and short stories should be double-spaced
- SASE for notification (.45 cents) plus additional postage for possible return of submission if desired
- Author's name & address at top of each page of paper copy and first page of e mailed copy.

Submit to:
Goose River Anthology, 2013
3400 Friendship Road
Waldoboro, ME 04572-6337
E mail: gooseriverpress@roadrunner.com
www.gooseriverpress.com